University of

Iowa Press

Iowa City

Elizabeth Oness

Articles of Faith

University of Iowa Press, Iowa City 52242

Printed in the United States of America

http://www.uiowa.edu/~uipress

 This is a work of fiction; any resemblance to actual events or persons is entirely coincidental. The publication of this book is supported by a grant from the National Endowment for the Arts in Washington, D.C., a federal agency.

Printed on acid-free paper

Cataloging-in-Publication data
on file at the Library of Congress.

ISBN 0-87745-726-3 (pbk.)

00 01 02 03 04 P 5 4 3 2 1

For Chad,

and for my sisters —

Patty, Terry, and Meg

And for the soul

If it is to know itself

It is into a soul

That it must look.

The stranger and the enemy,

we have seen him in the mirror.

—GEORGE SEFERIS

Contents

ACKNOWLEDGMENTS

I would like to thank the editors of the magazines in which these stories first appeared: "The Oracle" in *American Short Fiction*, reprinted in the *1994 O. Henry Prizes*; "A Confusion of Light" in *Witness*; "Rufus": the *Chicago Tribune* (Nelson Algren Prize), reprinted in *Glimmer Train*; "A Crescent in the Skin," under the title "Articles of Faith" in *Many Mountains Moving*; "The Music Underneath" in the *Hudson Review*; "Momentum" in *Crazyhorse*; and "Theodolite" in *Meridian*. "The Narrow Gate" was selected by Lynna Williams and Reynolds Price for second place in the Visions Short Story Contest and selected by Charles Baxter for the *1998 Painted Bride Quarterly* fiction prize.

The short story title "The Music Underneath" is indebted to the title poem of Jeffrey Harrison's collection *The Singing Underneath*.

The epigraph, taken from George Seferis's "Argonauts," was translated from the Greek by Rex Warner.

Blessed in friends, I received special help from these people during the years these stories were written: Debra O'Reagan, Donna Harrington, Kim Roberts, Claudia Booker, and Richard McCann. Thanks also to Trudy Lewis and Speer Morgan for their help. And Lainie Forman in memoriam.

Articles of Faith

The Oracle

I'd been home, out of college, only a few hours; I hadn't even unpacked the car, when my mother told me that she had met someone. He's a dentist, she said, and he's been saved.

"Saved from what?" I opened the refrigerator to survey its contents. Whenever I came home from school, the abundance of her refrigerator amazed me. At school, the staples in our refrigerator were ketchup, mustard, and beer.

"Saved?" I prompted her.

"Philip, don't be smart," she said.

"No, really, what brand of Christian is he?"

"Oh, I know it doesn't matter to you. But he told me about it on our first date, how everything's changed for him, how he gets along with his ex-wife now, and how he really feels like he's helping people, much more than fixing their teeth." She smiled a little as she repeated his happiness.

I had noticed a difference in her at graduation, but I thought it was relief that I'd made it through college unscathed. She seemed more relaxed, less precise. She no longer moved things and straightened them when she talked, a habit she picked up, or maybe I only noticed it, the year my father died. After the first months of mourning I waited for her to break out of herself, to become less restrained, but she continued in much the same way. She was a pretty woman with a small, square jaw, and long brown hair just starting to turn gray. Every year she asked if she should cut it, and every year I said no.

"Mom, I think you're in love," I said.

"Oh, I'm not," she smiled as she denied it, then set the plate she was holding back in the dishwasher.

"You don't even know if you're loading or unloading." I took the clean plate from the rack. "So he's divorced. Does he have kids?"

"He has a fourteen-year-old daughter who's just started to live with him again," she said. "And he's having a cookout tomorrow. He asked if you'd come, he wants to meet you."

Whenever she was flustered, my mother inspected some insignificant object as if its stillness would steady her. She examined the calendar on the kitchen wall as if it were new. I walked over and hugged her; she felt smaller, her rib cage like a brittle basket. I squeezed her lightly and released her. She looked up at me, reassured, and smiled.

The following night, on the way to his house, I tried to get her to describe Hal. She blushed and said I would meet him myself. It was strange to see my mother fidgety over a man. As far as I knew, in the years since my father's death, she had never even been out on a date. Of course her friends encouraged her to get out more, meet someone else, but she always refused. This devotion to the memory of my father was antiquated, probably even wrong, but my mother would not be pressed about things she didn't want to do. She had the ability to summon a formality that kept people from pressing her further. We drove through a wooded development, winding down smoothly paved roads with those peculiarly feminine suburban names: Natalie Court, Caroline Lane. We finally stopped in front of a large, modern house. Wind chimes hung from a Japanese maple in the yard. A slender window divided the house; starting by the front door, it rose up to the second story. Hal opened the door before my mother had a chance to knock.

"Hello, Deirdre." He kissed her on the cheek and turned to me.

"Philip, it's a pleasure. I've heard a lot about you." He shook my hand firmly. It was a humid day, but Hal seemed freshly scrubbed, as if he'd just stepped out of the shower. His light crew cut was edged with gray; his blue eyes were pale-lashed, rimless. A large gap separated his two front teeth. No wonder he was a dentist.

We walked through the house, which shone with polished wood floors and sleek, modern furniture, and into the kitchen, where the back wall, almost entirely glass, looked onto a lush backyard. Hal guided my mother through the doors, placing his palm against the small of her back. His fingers were short and thick. Peasant hands, my father would have called them. He started to lead us down to a small group of people standing around the grill when a young woman, dressed entirely in black, walked over.

"Philip, this is my daughter Megan," Hal said.

It didn't seem possible she was only fourteen. I was careful with my eyes; I tried to stare only at her face.

She smiled briefly and brushed her hair from her cheek. A clutter of black plastic bracelets and silver chains slid down her arm.

"Philip just graduated from University of Virginia," Hal told her.

"How impressive." She wrinkled her nose at me.

Hal looked uncomfortable.

"Deirdre, you look nice." Megan kissed the air near my mother's cheek. Her lips puckered, then relaxed into their fullness. It wasn't your usual fourteen-year-old gesture. I later came to associate those airy kisses with girls I'd known in college—when I ran into them many years later. Women I'd never touched would greet me with that pressure on the arm, a softness aimed at my ear.

"Would anyone like a drink?" Megan asked.

"I'd love a beer," I said.

Megan went into the house and my mother and Hal joined the group at the grill. I lingered awkwardly, waiting for Megan. She returned with two tall-neck beers and nodded at our parents.

"Well, what do you think?" she asked.

"About what?"

"About them." She gazed at me, unblinking. She had light gray eyes, darker near the pupils. She seemed to be deciding if I was playing dumb. "They really like each other," she said. "My father keeps hinting they might get married."

"I just got back yesterday." I wanted to defend my ignorance. "I'm trying to take it all in." Then cautiously I said, "My mother says your dad's been saved."

She snorted and looked across the lawn at Hal, who was talking to his friends, one arm gesturing, the other around my mother's shoulders. Megan took a long drink of beer. I wondered if he let her drink or if she was just showing off.

"Yeah, he's been saved all right," she said.

"What about you, have you been saved?"

"Hell no," Megan laughed.

"What do you believe in?"

"Oh, I don't know." She twisted up her mouth, chewing on the inside of her cheek. Her hesitation made her seem closer to her age.

"What do *you* believe in?" she asked.

"Elliott's," I said.

"What?"

"Elliott's Apple Juice. It has little quotations written on the inside of the caps."

She shook her head.

"I meditate for an hour every morning before I choose my first bottle." I leaned closer, lowered my voice. "I believe in the cosmic synchronicity of my choosing a particular quotation. I live every day by the wisdom inside a bottle cap—unless I drink two bottles; then I have to change my whole philosophy in the middle of the day."

She laughed, then looked at me sideways to make sure I was kidding.

"It's as good a thing to believe in as any, I suppose." She looked out over the yard. She was one of those girls who tried to look bad, but couldn't really pull it off. Her hair was cut in bangs and fell just below her ears, a stylish cap of dark hair that showed off her long neck. She affected the attitude of a streetwise flapper, but her face gave her away. Her cheeks were slightly round, child-like; she had a sprinkling of freckles. Megan. It was hard to be tough with a name like that. Her black T-shirt, cut wide and ragged around the neck and cropped along the bottom, ended a few inches below her breasts and stayed out there, not tucked into anything. I wanted to slide my hand up underneath it.

"I have to make a phone call." She turned abruptly and walked toward the house.

My mother introduced me to the other guests. We listened to a tall woman with waving arms tell an elaborate story that turned out to be a movie plot. A man in camouflage pants talked to Hal about target practice and a new rifle he'd bought. I ate food as it was handed to me. I was aware of the dark smell of charcoal, Megan's bare shoulders, scents of dark and light circulating through the blue evening. Hal worked his way around to my mother and me.

"So you had a chance to talk to Meg?" he asked.

"Yes," I said. "She seems quite grown up."

Hal looked at me hard, trying to decide what I meant.

"I hear you did well at school, magna cum laude. Maybe you can encourage Megan. She's bright, but she doesn't apply herself."

I nodded and tried to look understanding. He was reminding me of her youth. I was afraid whatever I said would be wrong.

Later, as my mother prepared to leave, I watched Hal draw her over to him, circling his arm around her waist, so that both of them could wish his friends good-bye.

"Did you have a good time?" Megan's question startled me.

"Not exactly my type of party," I said.

"What is your type of party?" Her voice was low, flirtatious.

"I don't know." I stumbled, afraid her father would hear her tone if not her words.

"Well, I'm sure we'll be seeing each other again." She looked at me, wide-eyed, from under her bangs.

Washington, D.C., was a tropical city in the summer. The sky could threaten rain all day, and after it finally poured, the air was still thick and hot. I spent that summer working on my résumé, studying the classifieds, and meeting with alumni who worked for companies I might be interested in. I felt like I was moving into a borderless cloud. I drank apple juice, hoping for clues to my future. In my cap one day:

> There is only one success—to be able to spend your life in your own way.
>
> —Christopher Morley

I had no idea what my own way was. I went out at night with friends who were in the same postgraduation haze. I read the *Washington Post* completely, every morning, as if one day I would find in its pages the exact thing I was meant to do. I thought about Megan almost constantly. I tried not to. I thought about her when I woke early in the summer heat, filled with the shadows of my dreams. I thought about her at night, too: her mouth, the way she put a bottle to her lips. I tried to imagine living in the same house with her. I imagined her getting out of the shower, walking past my room in a towel, wet.

My mother occasionally asked about girls I'd gone out with at college, but her questions were random; she might have been asking about a professor, or a difficult course I'd taken. I assumed she didn't want to know anything too specific, my answers might embarrass her, so she ironed my shirts and asked about my interviews, which weren't real interviews at all, but a series of talks with men who had established specific places for themselves in the world. I looked forward to weekends, when I wouldn't have to answer her questions; but when I woke up alone, sunlight filling my room, the house silent below me, it seemed that Hal had everything in that glassed-in house several miles away: he and my mother eating brunch in the kitchen, Megan upstairs sleeping late. I imagined her face, flushed with sleep and creased a little from the pillow, her smooth hair awry. I wanted her before she put on her grown-up edginess; I imagined her arms around my neck, how she would curl her long legs around mine. I tried to picture exactly what she looked like under those flimsy clothes, and I lay in bed for what seemed like hours, wondering whether she was a virgin or not. I fantasized until I exhausted myself. Then I slept, and when I woke, I tried to think of how I would distract myself for the rest of the day.

One Saturday morning my mother called from Hal's and asked me to dinner. I'd just gotten up and I stood in the kitchen, listening to her on the phone while I waited for the coffee to finish dripping. It was strange to be invited to another man's house by my mother. Driving over that night, I thought about Hal; my opinion of him shifted slightly each time we met. That night he seemed confident, self-sufficient, but there was an odd difference between him and my mother, as if they were the right and left shoes of a slightly mismatched pair. Hal insisted on cooking, as if his kitchen wasn't my mother's territory yet. When he moved around the table serving us, I watched his reflection in the large window. He was substantial, squarely built—each of his polo shirts was the exact same tightness across his chest—but he seemed like a pasty shadow superimposed over my memory of my father, a dark, transparent man of air.

Megan hurried into the kitchen and grabbed an apple off the counter. She wore a short black skirt, high-topped sneakers, and a long T-shirt. She moved as if she hadn't grown into her body yet.

"What's the hurry?" Hal asked.

"I told you, I'm going to the movies with Jill."

Hal stopped for a moment, holding a dripping spoon above a pan.

"I asked you last week. It's *Gone with the Wind.*" Megan's tone was highly reasonable, as if she were talking to a child. "We went through the whole thing about how it's a long movie, remember?"

Hal smiled, but his tolerance seemed strained.

"What about dinner?"

"Mmm, lasagna. Save some for me. Don't let Philip eat it all." She grinned at me and hurried out the door.

At home that night, I sat in front of the television, flipped through all the channels twice, and turned it off. I tried to remind myself what I'd learned about women in the past few years. I found that the girls who dressed most wildly, who seemed so sure of their looks, often wanted talk more than sex. Of course you could never be sure, but it was the straight ones, those preppie girls in button-down shirts who seemed a little awkward, shy even—those were the ones who had their diaphragm in their purse.

"So has Hal decided what he thinks of me?"

My mother and I were sitting in the kitchen. I'd made dinner, spaghetti with clam sauce, because she seemed tired and I'd had another long week that added up to nothing. My mother managed a print shop in Bethesda. They did stationery, fliers, advertisements; it was not a bad job, but it was hectic at times. The owner kept saying he was going to retire and leave my mother in charge.

I bought a bottle of wine for dinner, although my mother didn't usually drink. I poured a glass for each of us, and when she gestured for me to stop at a small amount, I kept pouring. I missed this hour at school, sitting on the porch with a few beers, grumbling about professors, telling stories or lies, and watching the sun go down over the Blue Ridge Mountains.

"I need a new dress for church on Sunday," she said.

"You're going to church?"

"I've been going for a few weeks." She twirled her spaghetti on a spoon and took a large bite.

"What's it like?"

"It's fine."

"It's church, of course it's fine. What's it *like*?"

"Well, it's a regular service, but everyone seems very sincere. It's a little embarrassing. When they pray they sort of raise their hands in the air." She showed me, raising one arm, then the other almost shyly, her open palms in a gesture of supplication. "Sometimes," my mother started to giggle, "they only raise one hand, like asking to be called on in class."

"Does Hal do that?"

"No," she said, relieved. "But it's strange. Sometimes I wonder if there's something wrong with me. I don't feel anything." She smiled a little, lightened by her admission, and tapped her glass for more wine. She had made two completely uncharacteristic gestures, the raising of her palms, tapping her glass for wine. The unnatural movements made her seem younger, confiding.

"The thing is," she hesitated, "it's important to Hal, he wishes I were more interested. I don't mind going, but . . ."

"But what?"

"I guess if I were more involved, he would be more sure of me, somehow. Of course he's never said it like that, but . . ."

I looked out the window. The sky was pale behind the trees. "If he really loved you, he'd want you either way," I said.

"I suppose." She sighed and picked up her plate.

The next morning my mother announced that she and Megan were going shopping.

"You and Megan?"

"Hal said he'd buy her some clothes if she'd get something that wasn't black."

When Hal's car pulled in the driveway, I picked up the newspaper as if I hadn't been waiting. My mother answered the door, and I heard her and Hal making plans for later on. Megan's shoes clicked across the kitchen floor. I listened to her opening up the cabinets and getting something to drink. When my mother went to get her purse, Megan came in and sat down next to me.

"So you and my mother are going shopping?"

"My father set it up, he wants us to be friends." She said it evenly, as a statement of fact. When she looked around the room, I thought how small our house seemed. She leaned back and stretched, looking up at the ceiling. I wanted to run my finger along the tendon at the back of her knee.

"But I do like your mother, she's a good person, innocent in a way."

"Innocent?"

"She always believes the best about people."

It surprised me, her saying this. It was true. My mother always had a theory to account for someone's bad behavior. Serial killers, rapists, thieves, she believed that, given enough time, a person's goodness would ultimately rise to the surface. I'd never known whether to call it optimism or foolishness.

When they left, the house seemed drained. I picked up a novel and put it down. The oak wall clock ticked louder, almost faster, as if it might rattle the china in the cabinet below.

My mother returned with a whole outfit—a skirt and blouse made of pale brown cloth with brightly colored threads running through it. A loose-fitting vest went over the top.

"They're wonderful for you." Megan grinned and held them up against my mother.

"Do you think your father will like them?" My mother touched the cloth with her forefinger.

"He'll like anything you wear." Megan's voice was encouraging. She took a soft purple belt from the bag and playfully dropped it over my mother's head.

"What about you?" I asked.

"He said he'd pay for whatever I wanted as long as it wasn't black and it didn't show my navel." She pulled out a pale green shirt made out of silky cotton. "It's kapok, it's made out of milkweed—the way it hangs is terrific." She stared at me, daring me to imagine her in it, then held it up, turning it around. "Backless. It looks great on."

Then, finished with me, she hugged my mother and thanked her for being so sweet, for taking her shopping.

A few days later my mother asked me to have dinner with her and Hal. She asked in a careful way that hinted it was important.

"Is Megan coming, too?"

"I don't think so," she said.

"She likes you." I remembered Megan hugging my mother.

"The divorce was hard on her. Hal's had a little trouble with her, but they seem to be working it out. It was a big step for her to move in with him."

"What kind of trouble?" I asked.

"Oh, that's not for me to say."

"Mom, if you're going to start, I wish you'd finish."

"I only said it's been a bit difficult."

My mother could be annoyingly proper. She didn't gossip. What had Megan done? Drugs? Possibly. Gotten pregnant? Too young. Well, not technically. I went round and round in my head. Imagining the possibilities made me jealous.

When Hal came to pick us up for dinner, Megan wasn't with him. He opened the car door for my mother, touching her arm as she got in. I slid into the backseat, watched the blur of fast-food restaurants and chain stores as Hal maneuvered down Rockville Pike, neatly cutting through traffic, a few aggravated horns honking behind him. When we climbed out of the car, heat rose up off the pavement, matching the heat in my head. Inside the restaurant, nets and fake sea memorabilia were strung along the walls. The smell of fish and melted butter made me hungry. Hal asked about the job hunt. I recited my growing list of dead ends.

"Well, it's hard to know what you want to do. I didn't decide to be a dentist right out of college."

"What did you do when you graduated?" I asked.

"I went to California, surfed for a while, then I went to Alaska. I had this romantic notion about working there, but the emptiness drove me crazy, so I came back and joined the service. I knew they'd pay me to train me."

"Why did you choose being a dentist?" I asked.

"I was good with my hands. I could talk to people, and I figured if you have to work, you might as well make money."

I liked his honesty if not his reasoning. Over the meal we talked about work and school. He mentioned shooting, and I asked a few questions about skeet shooting. It seemed that I'd been having the same conversation for weeks. Finally, Hal took a drink of water and aligned his silverware next to his plate.

"I just want you to know that I love your mother very much. She's a rare woman. I also want to tell you that I've come to God in the past few years. He's the center of my life. I know that each person comes to Him in their own way, and I don't ever want you to feel that I'm pushing you when I express my feelings about the Lord."

I couldn't look at my mother. His honesty was painful. I felt myself blush.

"Well, I appreciate you talking to me," I said.

"I also want you to know that you're always welcome at the house. Don't worry if it takes you a while to find the job you want. I know you're a real self-starter. Be picky about that first job." He took my mother's hand and squeezed it.

"Thank you."

I reached for my wine glass. It was empty and I lifted it up, feeling that Hal's words called for some comment, but I had nothing to say. I felt the silence as my arm came down. There was only a single glass of wine left and I didn't want to pour it for myself. Hal did it for me.

"And Megan looks up to you. Don't worry if she acts smart. She has a little growing up to do."

"She's a lovely girl," I said, feeling myself redden.

The waitress returned with coffee, and our conversation floated back to the surface.

I woke the next morning knowing that Megan was out of the question. I had to stop thinking about her. Finding a job so I could afford my own apartment was the only way out. At eleven o'clock I had an appointment at World Bank with the father of an old roommate. Getting ready to leave, I looked myself over in the mirror and felt better. I would get a job and get my own place. I bought an apple juice when I got off the Metro, and my bottle cap confirmed me:

> For he who has no concentration, there is no tranquillity.
> —Bhagavad Gita

I was shown into an office that looked like a private library. The walls were filled with bookcases, oil paintings, and photos of Paul's father shaking hands with important people. A set of golf clubs rested in the corner. Paul's father gestured toward a leather armchair. A secretary appeared in the doorway to ask if I wanted coffee. When she shut the door behind her, the hum of air-conditioning sealed us in. After looking at my résumé and asking a few questions, he let me know that my background was mediocre, that studying French meant practically nothing. I should have studied Spanish, German, Japanese, or Russian, those were the important languages. I listened to his polite advice and excused myself as quickly as I could.

Down on the sidewalk, I watched the people hurrying by and I wondered how it was that they all had something specific to do. A bicycle messenger wove down the sidewalk and through the standing traffic; pedestrians flattened themselves against solid objects and glared in his wake. I took off my tie. I was wet through to the back of my suit. At the entrance to the Metro, a man with no legs was propped up on a cardboard square. He held out a paper cup, and I glared at him and stepped onto the moving staircase.

When I walked in the front door, the house seemed small. I looked at the photographs of me growing up, my mother and father; they seemed at once familiar and generic. The house was still. I went to take a shower, to wash the morning off, and when I got out, the phone was ringing.

"Hi, Philip. Is your mom there?" It was Megan.

"She's at work. Do you want me to give her a message?" I didn't want to let her off the phone yet.

"No." She was quiet for a moment, then her voice picked up. "Well, I guess you had the God talk last night."

"Well, there wasn't a whole lot of discussion."

Megan giggled. "Look, do you feel like going into the city, just walking around or something? I want to get out of the house."

"Sure." I said it before thinking.

"Great. Come by in about half an hour, okay?"

I tucked the towel around my waist and went to get dressed.

"So what did he say last night?"

We were driving toward D.C. without a specific destination. I was aware of being in the same small space with her. She leaned against the car door, her knees tipped toward me. "Come on, what did he say?" she asked again.

"He said that he loved my mother a lot, and he talked about

how important church was, all that." I was too embarassed to repeat the words he'd used.

"That's all?" she asked.

Megan directed me as we got closer to the city: turn here, go left up there. It was funny the way she ordered me around. We parked in Adams Morgan, an old Hispanic neighborhood now gentrified with restaurants, record shops, and bars.

"I'm starved," Megan said. "I know a Mexican place that's cheap, and they make terrific margaritas."

She led me down the shopping street into a seedy part of town. A runny-eyed woman shared a stoop and a bottle with two men. On the corner, a check-cashing store was crowded. The restaurant was empty except for a Mexican family in the corner. The dim quiet was soothing; we were hidden from the daily world. Megan explained how she'd found the restaurant, but I didn't always pay attention to her words. I watched her mouth, her long fingers, ten perfect crimson dots at the tips. The icy lime and salt blended in my mouth, became warm in my stomach. Megan ate slowly, fishing around in the salsa for bits of tomato.

"I can't wait to go to college," she said. "No one around to watch what you do."

"Is it better living with your father?"

"Dad's weird, Mom's weird, it's kind of a trade-off." She stirred her drink, wiping salt down into the slush.

"How did your dad die?" she asked.

The question surprised me.

"He had cancer. One of the kinds you're supposed to survive."

"How old were you?"

"Thirteen."

"It's a rough age to have that happen," she said.

I laughed out loud. Her expression shifted from concern to anger.

"What?" she demanded.

"Rough age, as if you're the voice of experience."

"You don't have to be any special age to know things." She stared at me and sat back in her chair. Then she looked off at the mural on the wall. The slight roundness under her chin trembled.

"I'm sorry."

She crossed her arms and looked away. "Never mind," she said. "Maybe we should go."

"I really am sorry."

"Then pay." She leaned over the table and pushed the check toward me.

We left and walked into the late afternoon sun. I wanted to touch her, to cup my hand around the nape of her neck. We strolled down the shopping street, and, as we stopped to look at some of the more bizarre store windows, I felt her anger ease.

On Columbia Road we turned west and sat down near a playground at the top of the hill.

"Do you think being saved has really changed him?" I felt philosophical; drinking sometimes made me think about God.

We looked out over the playground. The sky was pink and orange behind the apartment buildings that bordered the park. Two chubby little boys started to fight over a plastic tractor.

"He's changed all right, but he had to. He got caught. And he's sorry." Her voice was bitter.

"He got caught?"

She paused, weighing something.

"He needs to make something out of everything. He couldn't have all the ruckus and just go on his merry way. He had to do something positive." She sneered when she said "positive."

"Positive?"

"Yeah." She kicked her foot against the wall. "Jerk. Once I got a really good report card—all A's except one B. My dad has always been real big on grades, and I was so excited that I went over to his office right after school, which is something I never did. The waiting room was empty, so I went back to where the offices were, and no one was there. I started to feel scared, everything was so quiet. His office door was closed, but I heard sounds of moving behind it, so I walked up to the door to knock on it, and then I heard a woman's voice, little sounds, then not-so-little sounds. They got faster and louder, and I just stood there, listening. Finally they stopped and I heard my father's voice and a woman giggle and I just turned around and left."

"How old were you?"

"Eleven, twelve, I guess."

"You didn't tell anyone?"

"No, my mother found out some other way."

My stomach felt as if I'd hit a sudden bump in the road. I thought about my mother, wondered if he would do that to her.

"So when all this got found out, that's when he got saved?"

Megan nodded.

She put her arm around my waist. Then she leaned against me and I slid my hand down her arm, smoothed her hair.

"I'm sorry," I said.

"You had nothing to do with it." She sounded mad, as if she were going to cry.

"I just mean I'm sorry it happened."

"Well, things happen all the time. I still think my father's a jerk. And I hate all this Christian shit. I know the reason for it."

"But you said you think he's really changed."

"I think he has. That's why I'm mad, too, because he feels all better now, and I still feel like a kid standing outside his door with my stupid report card, listening to him fuck his hygienist."

Our arms were still around each other and I was suddenly aware of my limbs, as if I were singing in public and I had to decide what to do with myself. I held her lightly, unsure of what to say. Two teenage girls with bright shopping bags walked by, and I imagined Megan at twelve—standing outside a door, her face pale and freckled under the fluorescent lights, listening to her father and his nurse. I rubbed her arm, but she ignored me and stared out over the playground. I bent to kiss her shoulder, she turned and studied me, then she slid her arms up around my neck and kissed me, a little shyly at first, then not shyly at all. We stayed like that for a long time, talking and kissing until dark.

When I walked in the door, my mother was watching TV with the lights out. Usually she read, curled up in a chair with her feet underneath her. The blue light deepened the lines in her face. A burst of canned laughter spilled out of the television. She asked how my interview went, and at first I couldn't remember what she was talking about. Then I remembered that morning and started to explain why it was lousy. Even in the dark I saw she wasn't listening, so when I said I met a friend for dinner, the lie came easily.

"Are you okay?" I asked.

"I suppose." Her voice was low.

"Did you and Hal have a fight?"

"I wouldn't call it a fight," she said. "I don't feel like talking about it now."

She forced a smile. I wanted to help her, but I was too full of Megan. When I kissed my mother's hair and said good night, she didn't move.

"Do you want me to turn off the TV?" I offered.

"No," she said.

I touched her arm and left her in front of the television.

I stretched out on my bed and thought about Megan, the way she tasted, the small sounds she made. I wondered what Hal had told my mother. I would have to say something to her, and I dreaded it.

The next day I was afraid that Megan would retreat into her prickly self, but when I called her, she suggested that we meet. Before we could arrange it Hal must have walked into the room, because her voice changed and she hung up.

The whole week was a series of interrupted phone calls and aborted plans. I couldn't pick her up because Hal's office was adjacent to his house and my car would be recognized. There were no buses in her neighborhood. I started to hate the suburbs.

I told myself that I'd talk to my mother after I saw Megan again. I put it off because I couldn't think of a way to say what I knew. Finally, one Thursday night, my mother came home early from dinner with Hal. She sat down in the kitchen and pulled off her shoes.

"Mom, did Hal tell you about his marriage, his divorce, and all that?" I tried to sound casual.

"Yes, he did." She was sorting through the mail, placing it in small piles on the table. The definiteness of her answer surprised me.

"What did he say?"

"That's between us, don't you think?"

I stood by the bulletin board, poking a large plastic tack in and out, making a circle of tiny, dark holes.

"Well, you've seemed kind of upset. I thought it might be something to do with that."

She looked up at me surprised.

"His first marriage has nothing to do with it. He's a much different person now, anyway."

Her words startled me, *much different now*.

"Is there anything I can do?" I didn't know what else to say.

"No, Philip," she smiled, weary. "It's really between us."

I stuck the tack into the wood molding and decided to go for a drive.

The following night Megan called after I'd come home from having dinner with some friends. She sounded as if she'd been crying.

"What happened?"

"My friend Barry was in a car accident."

"Is he alive?"

"He's in a coma."

"Do you want me to come over?"

"Yes."

"Where's your dad?" I asked.

"Out with your mother."

On the way to her house, it occurred to me that Barry might be an old boyfriend. I switched off the radio and rolled down my window. The night air was cool as I drove past the dense woods. Her front door was unlocked, and I let myself in. Megan was on the phone with another friend of Barry's.

When she got off the phone, she seemed calm, as if she had settled some question. Without saying a word she went to the refrigerator and poured two large glasses of wine. She wore the backless shirt she'd bought with my mother; the fabric fell in a deep loop that showed the curve of her waist, the indentation of her backbone, all the way down to the small of her back. She padded down the hall and I followed her long legs, shadowed in the dark. We lay down on her bed and I let her talk about what happened until she started to cry again. My heart was beating quickly, out of rhythm with her sorrow. I slid my hand up under her shirt and touched her very slowly and softly. She moved against me when I put my mouth to her breasts. I was afraid to ask my question, so I touched her and waited. When she unbuttoned my shirt, reached for my pants, I knew it would be all right, and the rest of our clothes came off quickly, awkwardly.

I looked down at her face, the slope of her shoulders, her flattened breasts pale in the half-dark. Her mouth was open but she made no sound. She moved with me, but her motions seemed more a mirror of mine than her own. I slid my arms up under her knees. Her body was pliant, but she was somewhere far away, somewhere only in herself. I waited as long as I could before letting go.

Afterward, dozing, everything inside me settled into place. Then I heard voices in the living room, my mother and Hal. I started awake, sweating. I strained to hear what they were saying. What if they found me here? Then I remembered my car in the driveway. They already knew. My stomach felt like it was being squeezed by a cold hand. I heard Hal's voice, loud and angry in the living room and I looked at the clock by Megan's bed—1:35. Megan lifted her head from the pillow and heard them. She cursed under her breath.

We lay still for a moment, then she threw back the covers and got out of bed.

"What are you—"

She took the chair from her desk and placed it under the doorknob.

"I don't want him bursting in here," she said.

The air ticked behind my thoughts. I thought of Hal talking about target practice; I wondered if he had a gun.

"He is going to kill me," I said.

"No, he's not. Besides, it's nothing he hasn't done himself."

I couldn't see her eyes in the dark, but her voice was bitter and calm.

We lay still. Hal was shouting in the living room, and then my mother's voice was raised back, something I hadn't heard in years. The front door slammed. I wondered if she'd take the car. Blood pounded in my ears. If she took the car and left me here, Hal would kill me. I was sure of it. I felt for my jeans on the floor and rattled my pockets. I had the keys.

Then my mother's voice again:

"Take me home."

"Drive your son's car home."

Her voice lowered. She must have told him there were no keys in it, reasoning with him.

Finally, they left. We lay still, listening, making sure they were gone. The house creaked. Outside, the trill of crickets and peepers shifted into high gear.

"What will he do to you?" I asked.

"He'll be furious, but he won't *do* anything." Her voice was quiet and defiant. "I'll just tell him I haven't been saved yet."

"You're not afraid of being left alone?"

"No, but you should go."

I tried to dress quickly in the dark, but my fingers felt stiff and uncoordinated.

Megan didn't dress. She got up with me and took the chair from underneath the doorknob. We stood by the door, and I slid my hands down her back, wanting to feel what I had an hour ago, but I was too nervous and shaky to feel her smoothness under my hands.

"I'll call you later in the morning."

"Okay, you better go," she said.

I hurried out to the car, keys in hand. It stalled once and my heart started to pound again, but it caught the second time and I pulled out of the driveway.

When I got home, my mother was waiting. She stood by the kitchen table; the part in her hair was crooked, her eyes were bright.

"You had to do it, didn't you?" she shouted.

"Mom, I wasn't trying to—"

"It really was the last straw, do you know that? The last straw, to come back to Hal's house and realize that you two are in bed together."

My mother focused on me as if I looked different than I had that morning.

"She's just trying to get at Hal. She doesn't care about you. I hope you know that. She's a confused young woman. She'd sleep with almost anyone if she thought it would hurt him."

My mother's mouth was dark, rectangular, as her shouted words floated out. I leaned against the doorjamb and looked past her; I couldn't see outside through the kitchen light's reflection. I remembered Megan's calm defiance, her efficiency as she set that chair under the doorknob, as if it were something she had practiced. I felt the connection of everything I wanted to believe was separate—Hal gently guiding my mother through a door, Megan moving underneath me in the dark. My mother stopped to catch her breath and her features settled back into what I knew.

A Confusion of Light

I knew it had happened when Arthur jumped out of his chair and grabbed me by the shoulders, turning me away from the television, but I turned back, I wanted to see, and finally, at that moment of looking back, I saw a large burst of fire flow upward out of a window, a huge gust of orange tipped with smoke, and then a section of the building started to cave in, slowly, like a movie we'd seen with Elaine years ago. The TV announcer sounded frightened, grave, and the sound of his words beat in my ears because time had finally released itself and nothing was hypothetical anymore. Not like that movie—it had some long, unfamiliar name, something Indian. I thought of watching it with Elaine, watching flowers unfold and cities crumble—all in time-lapse and slow motion—against an ominous and soaring music. Crisscrossing traffic patterns filled a grid of city buildings with blazing streams of light, and over and over the soundless demolition of buildings: a puff of smoke showing the burst from within, and then the slow, almost graceful collapse, as huge old apartment buildings, their windows so neatly lined up, swayed gently to one side, as if sitting down sideways before collapsing.

Arthur sank back down in his chair, tugging up his pant legs, and the neatness of his familiar gesture seemed so odd, and futile, because we both knew our daughter was inside the compound, that she had not chosen to come out.

They started to replay it even as it was happening. A tank bobbed up and down against the building, and then fire poured out, and a heat moved through me, through my whole body, *please, please, please,* I whispered to myself and Arthur looked over at me, but I didn't know exactly what I was asking for. I'd thought, when the time finally came, that I would scream, or cry, that something would shake loose inside me, but instead I stood, rooted in the middle of the carpet, watching the burning building as if I could stand to know what was happening inside.

It was as if the fire burned up everything I'd read in the past weeks—the kind of people who joined cults, their personalities, their neediness, their uncertainty about the world. I couldn't understand why Elaine was there. Those articles didn't describe her, although one thing I could see: she'd always been unnaturally literal-minded. We didn't raise her like that, it was just how she was, how she'd always been.

When she started kindergarten, she wailed whenever I tried to leave her. I don't think she understood that I could be apart from her and still exist. She clutched at my legs, pressed her small, shaking shoulders against my thighs and I just couldn't stand to leave her. I remember looking out the large plate-glass window that faced the playground, and finally I calmed her by telling her that I would come around and wave to her through the window before I went home. So every day, after I dropped her at school, I'd walk around to that window to wave, and Elaine would be standing in the corner of the classroom, her small, round face solemn and expectant, her tiny braids with their curling ends hanging down to her shoulders. She stood so quietly, gazing in front of her, as if my wave would release her.

Once, in a hurry, I simply got in my car and drove away. I must have been half a mile down the road before I realized that I had forgotten to wave good-bye, and feeling foolish, and a little panicked, I turned the car around and drove back to the school. I pulled the car into the lot and jogged around the corner to the window, and Elaine was standing there, waiting, her hands clasped in front of her, both feet inside one linoleum square. When she saw me come around the corner, she smiled her shy smile, raised one chubby hand to make a child's open and closed wave, then turned back to join the others in the busy classroom.

The TV screen shifted onto some sort of press conference. Men in suits. They kept talking about "the children," as if they needed the excuse of children to try to rescue anyone. Elaine went in right after Christmas. She had told us, over the phone, that she was going on a Christian retreat. While she was talking I pictured those Marriage Encounter decals I used to see around town, orange and yellow hearts twined together, some Catholic thing I think, and it just didn't occur to me that there would be any problem. But so much happens to children once they're away from you. In some ways you know them so well; the simplest gesture tells what they will not say. Even childhood friends of Elaine's—I can see in the way they push their hair behind an ear, by how they sit or stand, that they are tired, or frustrated, or about to give up. The trappings of adulthood: fingernail polish, jewelry, cigarettes, tattoos, these don't hide what a certain tilt of the head will let you know. But beyond this, there's everything you can't know unless they tell you.

We guessed something was happening with Elaine when she was living there in Austin, but I didn't want to pry, to be too motherly. Over the years that I tried to get pregnant, I made a lot of vows about what I would and would not do if God would give me a child. Bargaining with God is foolish at best, but it's all we're left with at times. I promised I wouldn't be overprotective, too cautious, if God would give me this one child. Of course, we make promises against what's most central to our nature. I know I didn't always keep them, why else would Elaine go clear to Texas for a job? But even with the vows I made over those six or seven years, it didn't seem we were likely to have a child at all. Nobody talked about it the way they do now; it was a secret, a failing between the two of you. Arthur was patient during those years, although after a certain point, I think he wanted to placate me more than he wanted a child. Sometimes I'd make him come home at lunch and we'd go upstairs to our bedroom, the sunlight on the coverlet unexpected because we both got up for work while the sky was still gray. Lying down, I'd close my eyes, and I saw orange behind my lids. Orange sun, orange fire. I closed my eyes in front of the TV. Nothing came through. Our only child. I had three miscarriages before Elaine took. *Took*. Funny word, but that's how it worked in my mind, like a plant you weren't sure would survive transplanting. *Took, hooked, took*, something holding on inside me; it sounded sure, rooted. I woke up one morning and somehow knew that she would stay and I would have a child.

When she first moved to Austin, everything seemed fine. She got a job as a secretary at a big company, and she called home to talk about her office, the people she was meeting, the clothes she was buying for work. But after a few years, I guess it seemed like less of a novelty; maybe she started to regret not going to college. We told her we would help her, and she started taking classes at night, but after that, when I heard her voice on the phone and asked how she was doing, her answers were evasive, maybe a little embarrassed, although about what I couldn't say. I told myself she must be tired; her voice sounded thin, and I thought how conscientious she was, guessed she was trying to do too much. It's funny that none of the things I've read about people who join cults seem to apply to Elaine. They all said that people were lost, or looking for something, and well, aren't we all, but Elaine was so orderly, so factual and accountable, none of this seemed like the kind of thing she would do.

We went down to visit for her twenty-second birthday, and there was something about her that was too determinedly cheerful. The apartment was neat and clean; she'd obviously straightened up for us, and there were new foods in the refrigerator: tofu and tempeh, carrot juice. She had sold her bed and slept on a futon; I kept getting tofu and futon mixed up.

So when she called a few months ago and said she was going on this Christian retreat, I'd almost been relieved. We'd never been churchgoers ourselves, Easter and Christmas at most. And for a while I thought that might have been the problem: if we'd raised her one particular way, none of this would have happened. But it turned out that lots of the people in there were raised Christian, so there's just no telling.

I opened my eyes and saw the fire. I closed my eyes and saw orange. All that sun in making her, her conception a confusion of sunlight.

Arthur was pressed back in his chair. I wanted to say something, but I couldn't speak. I stared at that ugly building going up in flames and tried to picture Elaine. I couldn't. I held the arms of my chair and closed my eyes. Pictures, I told myself, you have pictures of her. It seemed impossible that I couldn't see her face at that moment. I tried to imagine her at our last visit, or even at sixteen, a tentative young woman, but all I could recall was her round, child's face, looking out at me through that large schoolroom window, her gaze fixed, knowing that I would come, knowing that my wave would release her.

Rufus

A friend of Jonathan's had given him the car when he returned to the United States. It was a dented, gray Toyota with primer silvering the extensive rust and doors that didn't lock. After a year of traveling through Asia and New Zealand, Jonathan had returned to D.C. broke, and he found it an unexpected sign of adulthood that a friend his own age could afford this generosity. The doors that didn't lock hardly seemed to matter—until he found Rufus living in his car. Actually, Rufus didn't live in the car, he slept in it, but it seemed like the same thing. Jonathan's apartment was a few blocks from the men's shelter on Fourteenth Street, and he guessed that Rufus got his meals there. He didn't like to ask too many questions; somehow it seemed that the more he knew, the more responsible he was, that asking too many questions was like feeding a stray cat.

Jonathan found him in his car on a rainy night in October, a night when he was expected at his prospective in-laws for dinner. He opened the door of his car, then jumped back, startled by a substantial black man, in a paisley polyester shirt and a John Deere cap, sitting in the driver's seat, reading the newspaper. The man slapped the pages together and stared for a moment at the young Chinese man staring in at him. The scent of cologne floated into the damp air.

"Excuse me," Jonathan said. "What's going on here?"

"Just getting out of the rain." The man started to fold up his paper. His hands trembled as he aimed the newspaper's folded end at the side pocket of his blue vinyl Pan Am bag. With the paper secure, he braced one hand against the steering wheel and pulled himself around. "It's about dinnertime anyway." The man worked his jaw sideways as he guided his feet out of the car door. His square face sagged, as if the roundness of his cheeks had slipped down to his jowls.

Rain pelted the shoulders of Jonathan's jacket and he felt a few cold drops slide down inside his collar. He waited silently, holding the door like a chauffeur. When the man got clear of the car, he turned and shuffled away. His wide, high hips were crooked, flattened underneath.

Jonathan got into his car, dropping down too hard. The man had moved the seat back. He checked the glove compartment: registration, insurance, nothing was missing. Before pulling out, he looked in the rearview mirror and saw the man set his bag on the hood of a parked car; he bent over the bag and reached into it, fishing for something.

Now he would be late, and Pamela's parents would smile as they wordlessly telegraphed their disapproval. He had always felt uneasy around them. Although Pamela still denied it, her parents had been visibly surprised when they discovered he was Chinese. At their first meeting, Mrs. Wallace's brittle gaiety couldn't hide her discomfort; she touched the softly lined skin of her neck and exclaimed about everything he said as if it were startlingly new. Pam's father offered him wine and inquired about his parents with a grave delicacy. Jonathan told them that his father, an American, was an attorney in San Francisco, and his mother, who lived in D.C., was an acupuncturist who treated drug addicts. They had heard of his mother; she was frequently written up in the newspapers. Jonathan tried to keep the conversation from lingering on her work; he found it hard to talk about his mother without making her sound eccentric. Pam's father seemed reassured to know that Jonathan had graduated from a prestigious university in the Northeast. Their genteel formality made Jonathan imagine himself boisterous, raising his glass and saying, "Well, what do you think the kids will look like?" Instead, they all held their wine glasses by the stem and spoke slowly. Pamela sat next to him and basked in her parents' approval when he mentioned his acceptance at SAIS, the School for Advanced International Studies in Washington, D.C. He imagined Pam's mother murmuring, *State Department*, over lunch to her friends. Ever since that night he felt that any Wallace family occasion combined the polite evaluation of a job interview with the ominousness of a doctor's appointment.

Since they'd become engaged, he felt even less at ease. He carefully avoided mentioning the neighborhood he lived in, one of the last renovated blocks east of Dupont Circle. Every day, Jonathan passed the men lined up outside the shelter. Some stood silently on the pavement, staring toward the head of the line; others smoked cigarettes and talked as any group of men might. One pale young man, with a fixed grin, often hopped around on the sidewalk, flapping his flannel-clad arms. Glimpsed for a moment, he might have been a man enjoying himself, telling a joke at a party, but the moment went on for too long, and the way he spun on the pavement made Jonathan think of a wobbling gyroscope. A slight man with wire frame spectacles often sat on the church steps reading a book in the late afternoon. He looked like a dutiful merchant, passing a quiet hour with a book. Another man costumed himself in various street trash, and Jonathan had recently seen him wearing a shaggy carpet toilet seat cover as a hat. He swept the pink mop off his greasy head, bowing to women in the street. "I salute you with my tiara," he said.

Jonathan assumed that the man he'd found in his car was simply disoriented; he'd discovered it unlocked and decided to wait out the rain. But the following week, when Jonathan opened his car door, he found the man sorting papers: odd-shaped scraps were neatly arranged along the dashboard, and four piles of bank statements and canceled checks had been placed in neat stacks on the passenger seat. Jonathan peered in at him and the man moved to cover his papers as if the wind would blow them away.

"Look, you just can't do this," Jonathan said.

"Sorry." He gathered up the piles and set them crosswise on top of one another. A cigarette burned in the ashtray.

"And I don't smoke, so I'd appreciate it if you wouldn't smoke in my car." Jonathan heard the edge of superiority in his voice and felt embarrassed; he sounded like a snotty kid. He also realized that he'd made a tactical error: by setting the boundaries of what he could and could not do, it sounded as if he were giving the man permission to use his car.

The man placed two of the smaller piles in a black address book. The leather was soft and shiny. He snapped a thick rubber band around the book to secure it, then put the other papers into his bag.

"Don't mean to hold you up, lost track of time." He got out of the car and straightened up slowly.

Jonathan watched him silently, trying to look stern, but the man wasn't looking at him so he didn't notice.

He was on his way to pick up Pamela, and when he got into his car, the lingering smell of cigarettes and cologne made him guess the man was spending a lot of time in it. Of course the logical step would be to move the car, but parking in Washington, set by zone, restricted him from moving it very far. He imagined the man searching for the car and finding it several streets away. He'd be ashamed of trying, and failing, to elude someone who was old and without a place to stay.

He'd been avoiding telling Pamela. Jonathan knew she'd have a decisive plan that he, in turn, would probably resist. Pamela had pretty, delicate features, and a high, wispy voice, but he had learned, early on, that her decisiveness was deeply ingrained. They had met two years ago, while she was studying for the bar exam. On their second date she'd made it clear that passing the bar was her main priority. He remembered her tone, as if she were expecting resistance, and when he told her that he'd been saving money for several years to take an extended trip to New Zealand and the Far East, he saw her redden slightly, and fumble with a bracelet she was wearing. He was attracted to that softness beneath her imperious tone. Something about the delicacy of her gestures, the way she always seemed to be in motion, made him think of moving water. He quickly discovered that the current running through her wasn't an abundance of energy, but a reluctance to be still, as if she needed to be busy to account for herself.

One night, after making dinner at his apartment, they went to bed, and in the interval between the first time they slept together and the time before he left, the balance of pursuit between them shifted. She seemed endlessly curious about him. In those first weeks, her questions about his growing up at the clinic, the years he'd spent in California with his father, made him feel as if the different parts of his past were beginning to coalesce. Usually he felt at the mercy of his environment. He was one person when he visited his mother at the clinic, and another when he was skiing with friends in Vermont. Pamela began to say how much she would miss him, and even though he liked to hear it, he was also glad that he would be away while she was preparing for the bar. She often woke up fretful, worrying about what she needed to study, as if his presence slowed her down. Her worrying, her need to accomplish things, was a trait that even her new vulnerability didn't ease; and so he had left, knowing she would probably be working in Washington when he returned, and that whatever was going to be between them would become apparent then.

In his absence she passed the bar, got a job with a large firm downtown, and her letters, arriving on corporate letterhead in China or New Zealand, were mostly filled with the news that she was working sixty hours a week, she was tired, she missed him, she was making money and had no time to spend it. Jonathan held these letters in his hand and looked out to the line of the horizon and the sea, the houses thatched with grass, and felt a strange sense of wonder that in some months he would return to Washington and his life would resume a distinct and linear course.

He told her about the man living in his car on a Sunday morning as they lazed over doughnuts and the paper.

"Why doesn't he sleep in the shelter?" she asked.

"I don't know."

"Well, ask him. Then tell him he has to find somewhere else to sleep. If you don't, he'll be living in your car all winter," she said.

All afternoon Jonathan rehearsed, to himself, different ways of asking the man not to stay in his car. He would be firm and logical, but kind. He would talk to him, explain. When he went to his car, the man wasn't there.

The following week the man was sleeping in the driver's seat, one arm draped over his Pan Am bag. Jonathan opened the door and touched his shoulder cautiously.

"Hey, wake up, I have to go," he said.

The man opened his eyes, then closed them for a moment and stretched. Jonathan felt annoyed by his leisurely waking.

"Look," he said, "don't you have anywhere else to sleep?"

"Would I be sleeping here if I did?"

"What about the shelter?"

"You ever spent the night in a shelter?"

Jonathan just looked at him.

"Don't mind eating there, but it's no place to sleep. Everybody's got knives, they try to steal my bag—nobody gonna take my bag. Dirty too. Junkies piss in the beds, piss in the corners. I like my whiskey, but I don't do no drugs."

Jonathan didn't know what to say. He stood in the street while the man shuffled near the gas pedal for his shoes, a pair of brown slip-ons with imitation metal horse bits on top.

"You can't keep sleeping in my car."

"All right, young man, I'll find myself another spot." Abruptly, he pulled himself out of the car. His shoes made a noise like slippers on the chilly pavement. When Jonathan slipped into the front seat, it was warm.

"What's your name?" Jonathan asked.

"Rufus. Rufus Williams."

Jonathan extended his hand through the window and they shook. Driving away, he hoped that Rufus would find somewhere else to sleep and that would be the end of it.

Two days later Jonathan found Rufus playing the radio in his car.

"You said you'd find somewhere else to stay."

"I tried." Rufus got out of the car and set his bag on the pavement. "I just haven't located myself yet."

"Well you have to find somewhere else. And you're going to run down my battery playing the radio like that."

They stood, facing each other. Jonathan imagined how Rufus must see him: a young Chinese man in his twenties, clean-shaven and well-fed. Jonathan reached into the car and snapped off the radio. Standing in the street, Rufus started to cry.

"You listen to me young man, I'm a veteran. I paid my way my whole life. I had the same apartment twenty-five years an' I paid my rent regular, but they got us all out 'cause they makin' it condos. I'm a veteran an' they put me on the street." He dug a handkerchief out of his pocket and wiped his eyes. "I got all my things in storage, two color TV's, big La-Z-Boy chair, but I got no place to put it."

"Don't you get a pension from the VA?"

"Hardly 'nough to live anywhere decent. Damn crackheads everywhere. I got cut visitin' my girlfriend last month."

His crying became a snuffling whine. Jonathan shifted his backpack, wishing he would finish.

"I know you got to use your car. I'm going down to the city to see about some Tenant Assistance Program. See where I am on the wait list. I used to have two cars, used to have a big old Caddy, wouldn't want someone sleepin' in that."

The next evening they had a party to attend in Arlington. Pam was in a good mood, fussing over the wrapping for a birthday present, teasing him. She wore a short red dress, not too fancy, but the kind of dress that inspired him to open doors for her, help her with her coat. When Jonathan opened his car door, he saw Rufus leaning forward in the front seat, reading a paperback by the light of a street lamp.

"Evening." He greeted Jonathan. He marked his place carefully before putting the book in his bag and raising his bulk out of the car. Jonathan introduced them, and watched Rufus take Pam's reluctant, slender hand in his large one.

"Pleased to meet you, young lady." Rufus took off his cap.

"Are you living in this car?" Pamela's no-nonsense tone made Jonathan wince.

"I wouldn't call it living. I stay here when I can't find nowhere else."

"Well, a car's no place to live in winter," Pamela said.

"Can't argue with you there."

"You have to find somewhere more permanent to stay." Pamela pushed her hair back from her face; her gesture had the air of a challenge.

"She always do your talking for you?" Rufus looked at Jonathan and then back to Pamela. "Listen young lady, this's his car and we had this discussion, him and me. I don't see how it's any of your business. I don't like sleepin' in his car any more'n he likes it, but I'm tryin' to get myself located and there ain't much I can do. You got a ring on your finger? He ain't your husband, you got no legal claim on this car. This discussion between him and me."

Rufus shouldered his bag, gave Jonathan a steady look, and headed down the street toward the church.

Pamela got into the car and slammed the door, "I can't believe him, getting self-righteous about sleeping in your car! It smells disgusting in here. You should fix the door and get a locksmith to make a key."

Jonathan didn't answer.

"Jonathan?"

"Look, obviously I've thought about that."

"Well, do it."

"Pamela, has it ever occurred to you to look at this a little differently? I don't like having him in my car, but I have a bed to sleep in, and mostly I sleep with you—I have two beds at my disposal. How can I deny him my car on a cold night? I mean, of course it's annoying, but it's not like he prevents me from using the car."

"God, I can't believe you." Pamela crackled the sheet of directions. They drove out of D.C. silently, then navigated Arlington's turning suburban streets, looking for house numbers under yellow porch lights. Jonathan imagined Rufus going to his car and finding himself locked out. He would stand in the road with his blue Pan Am bag at his feet, yanking at the chrome door handle, impatient and bewildered.

At the party Pam told the story about Rufus several times. Her telling of it made Jonathan sound indecisive and ineffectual. She moved through the party in her red dress, her long legs picking her way around a few people sitting on the floor. Jonathan decided that he wouldn't discuss Rufus with her anymore, but a few days later, when she asked about him, he didn't feel like lying either.

"Just fix the lock and get a key made, will you? Pretty soon you'll have a damn hotel in your car; it's getting cold out there," she said.

Jonathan was making dinner at her apartment and he wasn't in the mood to argue. He stirred the tomato sauce and poured himself another glass of wine. He believed that it wasn't good to get mad while preparing a meal: it would turn the sauce or spoil the food. It followed that arguing over dinner wasn't good either.

"Will you take care of it before the end of the week?"

"I'll do it when I feel like it," he said.

"You don't take charge of things, do you realize that? You let everything drift along until it bumps into some sort of conclusion."

He swirled the wine in his glass and stared at her through the reddish tint. She was right, but he didn't necessarily think this was a bad way to live. It was the weakness implied that bothered him.

"You make me sound so spineless. Do you know there are religions, whole belief systems, based on the idea of action in nonaction, allowing things to come to their natural conclusion?"

"Spare me that Eastern bullshit. It's just an excuse for not doing anything about it."

"Listen, it's fucking cold out there. What's he going to do when he gets to my car and he's locked out?"

"He'll find somewhere else. He doesn't have much incentive to look for a place if he knows he can drink all day and crash in your car at night."

"He doesn't always drink. He reads." Jonathan was uncomfortably aware of a strange internal echo. This sounded like something his mother would say.

"I can't believe you're defending him," Pamela stood in the center of the room holding two cloth placemats, her anger suspending her motion toward the table. "You can't spend your whole life just working around things you don't want to deal with."

"You're always so right." Jonathan set down the knife he was holding. He thought of the night of the party, of Pam telling the story over and over. It had been humiliating and he had let her get away with it. "You seem to thrive on this, you know?"

"What?"

"Arguing—it seems you're in the right profession." He saw her flinch and knew the remark had hit home. He picked up his coat and walked out of her apartment, leaving the door wide open behind him.

He walked down Connecticut Avenue in the cool night air. How long had they been like this? Eastern bullshit. Underneath everything was that really how she felt? He knew that Pamela valued speed, efficacy; they had often talked about how they complemented each other. Walking down the street he realized that perhaps, without her knowing it, Pamela loved him for exactly what she criticized: he was malleable, easy to get on with. He would be in school, undisruptive, while she climbed the corporate ladder. What if he wanted to drop out of SAIS, move somewhere else? He tried to imagine it. Pamela would have a fit.

As he went over the argument in his mind, he remembered the disturbing feeling of echoing his mother's logic. He wasn't at all like her, but something in his reasoning had sounded implacable and familiar. The magazine and newspaper stories painted her as noble, but really she was just oblivious to the accepted way of doing things. It still amazed him that she and his father had ever been married. His father accomplished things by understanding the law, by knowing what series of precedents would allow him to position himself advantageously. His mother simply did things—without preparation, without money. Years ago, she had heard about a doctor in New York who was treating drug addicts with acupuncture. She took Jonathan out of school for a few weeks and brought him to New York City where he trailed around the hospital after her, watching her place needles on the lobes of people's ears. Some of the patients gazed at him curiously, others ignored him. He had never seen so many colors of people. When she and Jonathan returned to D.C., a growing group of jittery patients came and sat in the waiting room along with those who came to be treated for back pain or tennis elbow. When one of the other acupuncturists complained that the detox patients made the other patients nervous, his mother simply opened her own clinic. She wasn't bothered by the fact that her patients couldn't pay, that she and Jonathan lived in two small, makeshift rooms above the clinic. His mother had found her mission. When he was away at college, she'd taken to walking through the back alleys of Northwest D.C., quietly trying to convince people, mostly young girls, to come into the clinic for treatment. When he found out, he was furious with her, but she simply poured tea for him and smiled. "I do it in the daytime," she had said. "No one bothers me." He had not understood her at all then, but since returning from China, his sense of what was possible had shifted.

Now he was hungry. He'd bought a bottle of red wine to drink with dinner and he wished that he'd taken it with him. He looked in restaurant windows as he walked down the street, but he didn't feel like paying to eat by himself. He stopped and bought a half-dozen bagels and a container of cream cheese.

Walking past his car, he peered through the window. Rufus wasn't there.

"Lookin' for me?"

Jonathan turned to see him walking out of the alley. With a streetlight behind him, he looked kindly, paternal.

"I just got a bottle, like to have a drink?"

"Sure."

Jonathan got into the driver's seat and Rufus walked around to the other side.

"Woman trouble?" Rufus asked.

"How can you tell?"

"It's Saturday night and you got your dinner in a bag." He grinned at Jonathan and pulled a bottle of brandy out of a paper bag. Jonathan tried not to think about germs as he wiped off the top of the bottle. He didn't usually drink. A glass of wine every so often. He held the liquor in his mouth for a long moment before swallowing.

"Women like her are jest like little kids," Rufus said. "They push you just to see how far you'll go. All you gotta do is tell them you had enough. They squawk a little, but they learn."

"Pam's got a mind of her own."

"I can tell," he laughed. "You got to watch out for a woman who thinks she knows what's best for you—that's the worst kind." He paused, took a drink. "No, there's worse. A woman that drinks is worse."

"Didn't you say you had a girlfriend?"

"Quit her. She'd get all liquored up, insensible. When I had my place, I kept a lock on the liquor cabinet. I told her she could drink all the beer she want, but I kept that cabinet locked up 'cause she'd get into the good stuff and it'd be gone."

Jonathan took a long drink and looked out at the night; the city sky was orange.

"You ever been married Rufus?"

"Thirty-two years."

"You're kidding me," Jonathan turned to look at the outline of his Rufus's face against the night. This single fact seemed to alter his silhouette. Rufus had been married longer than he'd been alive.

"Yep, thirty-two years. Denise was a lovely woman. Didn't drink, went to church regular, we got along real fine. She died eleven years ago in June and I'm just glad she ain't around now, 'cause she was a woman who believed in keepin' a nice house. Ain't no way she could live in a car, on the street."

They talked and drank into a blurry hour of the night. The next morning Jonathan woke with his shoes on, fully dressed. When he sat up in bed, he couldn't think what had happened for a moment. His throat felt hot and dry. He moved slowly into the kitchen for a glass of water and found one bagel left in the bag. He vaguely remembered Rufus cutting bagels with a knife, spreading cream cheese, joking that cream cheese was like white girls—you could see what you were doing in the dark.

Jonathan sat on the sofa with a glass of water and tried to reconstruct the evening. The red light on his answering machine blinked. He was sure it was Pamela, angry or apologetic. He remembered Rufus talking about women pushing at you, and he smiled at the blinking light. Good. But his head started to pulse in time with the tiny light, and the hot tightness in the back of his skull crept forward over his ears. He tried to piece together his conversation with Rufus, and for a moment the undividedness of it spilled back to him, two men sitting in a car, talking about women. Thirty-two years. Rufus Williams had been married for thirty-two years. Now he would never get rid of him.

The phone rang and the sound seemed to press into his brain. He waited for the answering machine to rescue him. The caller hung up.

He didn't play back his messages until late in the afternoon. They were all Pamela, angry at first, then worried, then tearful. After a few calls, there were only dial tones.

He decided to let her stew for a while. When he finally did call, the following day, he told her that he was sick of being nagged at, and that it wouldn't be too difficult to find someone who was easier to get along with. The sound of his voice, still angry, surprised him.

"Will you come over later?" Her voice sounded teary.

"I have class until six o'clock. I'll come over then."

When she opened the door, he felt oddly formal. She offered him tea, and when he started to talk, she began to cry.

"We have to come to some agreement," he said quietly. "I don't want to have an ongoing argument about the way I live my life."

"I'm sorry, it just seems that—" she stopped herself.

She reached for him without saying anything else. He bent to kiss her and thought how this was the only thing that seemed uncomplicated between them. His fingers felt as if he were touching her through a thin layer of something cloudy, something she didn't see. They moved to her bedroom, but in bed, his mind was too busy. He was distracted by odd thoughts, the radio, fragments of their argument. He tried to concentrate; he imagined her red dress. And what for her must have seemed like a deferral to her pleasure, was for him strangely unconnected, as if he were observing her from a distance. Finally, he pulled away.

"This isn't right," he said.

"What?"

"That we fight and then do this."

"It's called making up." Pamela smiled.

"No, that's not what I mean."

"I was just angry the other night." Her voice was quiet, trying to soothe him.

"You were saying what you thought. Eastern bullshit. That's incredibly dismissive."

"Jonathan, I'm sorry. I was angry, I was being mean."

He pushed her hair back from her face. He didn't want to talk any more.

That night, Jonathan found an empty McDonald's bag in his car. He felt annoyed and wondered if Rufus was inviting his friends to use the car. The next morning he went to his car primed for a serious discussion with Rufus. When he opened the door, he saw Rufus's Pan Am bag spilled on the passenger seat. He scrambled through the contents: an old brown shirt, a toothbrush and comb, a girlie magazine—no wallet, no papers, no knife. He stuffed everything back inside and set it gently on the car floor. He felt as if he'd stumbled on a body. Had Rufus been mugged in the car? He hurried to school, sweating, and thought of what Rufus had said about the shelters. A friend at school suggested he call the VA hospital.

After class he found a pay phone and he waited as the operator transferred him between different units. He repeated his questions and waited on hold, suspended in a network of faint voices. Finally they located Rufus in intensive care: his condition was listed as stable. When Jonathan hung up the phone he felt relieved and a little sick.

After a few days, Jonathan started to worry. What if they discharged Rufus and he came back? The only thing worse than having a homeless man in his car would be having a sick homeless man in his car. He imagined carting Rufus around because he didn't have the heart to put him out on the street. He called again to ask about visiting hours.

"You're visiting him?" Pam's voice was shrill with disbelief.

"I just want to make sure they know he doesn't have anywhere to live. I don't want them to release him and have him end up in my car."

Pamela started to speak, stopped, then took a deep breath.

"Jonathan, visiting him is absurd. You'll just develop more of a . . . relationship with him. And then he'll be *more* likely to come back."

Jonathan turned to look out the window. He felt enormously tired.

"You usually take the path of least resistance. It would seem to be easiest to let him go," Pamela said.

"You make me sound like a fucking jellyfish. I'm just trying to avoid having him come back sicker than he is."

"You're acting out of liberal guilt and you should just stop. It's not your fault that he's homeless. Are you going to turn into your mother?"

"There's nothing I want less than to be like my mother. She's completely eccentric; I'm just trying to be decent. You know, Pamela, once you decide how you feel about something, all you think about is how you can make your point. You don't even consider another perspective."

Pam's lip quivered, "Is this how you're planning to live your life? You're broke, in graduate school, and you're going to encourage this man?"

"I just want to let someone know what his situation is."

"Fine." Pamela turned and walked into her bedroom.

Jonathan stood still. He imagined what it would be like not to have to explain or defend himself, not to expend any effort in understanding how their lives could mesh. He tried to think if he had anything in her apartment of value. He went to the hall closet, took his coat, and let himself out the door. He closed it quietly, finally, behind him.

The Washington Hospital Center was a vast complex of gray concrete buildings. The signs pointing to different roads and hospitals made him feel as if he were driving to an airport. He glanced around him as he walked in the front door—a TV in the lobby, people in wheelchairs, no one too frightening looking. At the information desk, he learned that Rufus was out of intensive care. As the nurse recited the directions to his room, Jonathan listened carefully; he didn't want to see anything he didn't need to.

He paused at the door of the unit. No one noticed him because no one seemed capable of lifting his head. The beds looked like half-prone chairs with canopies of tubes and bottles suspended over each one. In the near corner, a nurse with platinum-blonde hair was drinking coffee and eating a muffin.

"Ah, excuse me, I'm here to see Mr. Williams," he whispered.

"Rufus?" she smiled, "he's right over there."

"I'd like to talk to you for a minute first, if I could."

"Sure, honey," she pointed to an orange stool next to her. He liked the way she said "honey," not flirtatious, but reassuring. She was large and clean; he felt like a small child.

"I'm here because Rufus was living in my car. He has no place to go and I thought the hospital should know that. I don't want him to leave here and come back to my car."

"Of course not." She smiled at him as if this were just one of many small events in her day. "Mr. Williams is going to be here quite a while. As a matter of fact, he'll be having another operation in a week or two. He'll probably be up on the list for subsidized housing by the time he's ready to leave."

Jonathan stared at her for a moment; he felt amazed at some small order in the world.

He walked over to Rufus who seemed shrunken inside his skin. Tubes containing different colors of fluids were patched into his arms and his sides. He had no idea what to say. The nurse came up behind him.

"Look who's here Mr. Williams."

Rufus opened his eyes and smiled weakly. He tapped the plastic shell that covered his trunk. His head was set in a brace; he looked like a brown turtle with tubes.

"Look pretty funny I bet." His voice was a croaking whisper.

"Yes, you do," Jonathan said. There was no getting around it.

"Pinched a nerve in my neck," he paused. "An' somethin' else too."

Jonathan wasn't sure what to say about the "something else," if he should ask or not. "Well, they look like they're taking good care of you."

"Good TV," Rufus croaked.

Jonathan looked up at the large color TV suspended from the ceiling. "I should have brought you a present, but I forgot," he said. He sat down on the chair beside Rufus. There was a game show on TV, and the contestants, all fat and manic, bounced behind their lecterns like overexcited children. He was relieved when Rufus dozed off.

He picked himself up quietly and walked toward the door. He thanked the nurse, who smiled at him as if his visiting a man who had been sleeping in his car was the most normal thing in the world.

He hurried down the hall. In the elevator he had to wait for a man with tiny, shrunken legs to wheel himself in. Jonathan forced a thin smile; the man stared back, sullen.

In the lobby Jonathan fished for his keys in his backpack; the double glass doors seemed like a finish line. Inside the first set of doors was a brightly lit candy machine, and it seemed incongruous there for some reason. He stood in front of the bright assortment of candies and suddenly wanted to taste something very sweet. He dug in his pockets for change, chose a chocolate bar, and passed through the doors. Outside, he looked around him and realized the view was unfamiliar; it wasn't the way he'd come in. In the distance, beyond a parkway, a line of bare trees looked soft against the pale sky. He sat on a low concrete wall to get his bearings, to taste the sweetness in the cold morning air.

A Crescent in the Skin

Sometimes Terry imagined her answering machine was willfully silent, swallowing her most important messages. She pictured it swelling like a frog: the flat, rectangular box bulging into a convex shape, the lid popping open with the final suppressed call. She lay on her bed, a fold-out sofa, flipping through the *Village Voice*. She studied the Mind/Body/Spirit section, the Personals; she told herself to get out, see a movie, maybe the phone would ring if she stopped watching it. The small sounds of the building: heat knocking in the pipes, Mrs. Anderson shuffling in and out, George talking baby-talk to his poodle outside her door, were magnified by the phone's silence.

Finally she gave in, grabbed her coat, and walked the five flights downstairs. Three days ago she had been called back for a part in a movie—not a walk-on, a real part. On the brownstone steps she hesitated, tapped her fingers against her mouth. "This is stupid, the phone is not broken," she told herself. Damp cold seeped up through her shoes. She pulled her coat more tightly around her and ran to the pay phone on the corner. Through the scratched plastic, she saw cloudy people hurrying against the wind. After four rings, her own voice answered; filtered through machinery, she sounded businesslike, serene. She dropped the receiver into the cradle and stared out into the street. The city was littered with tired Christmas decorations and slush.

The past few days kept playing over in her mind. She had been in the shower when they called. The phone rang and she had turned to let the hot water run over her face. She imagined it was someone from the restaurant, calling because another waitress hadn't shown up, but then she heard a crisp, unfamiliar voice leaving a message on her machine, and she jumped out of the shower and fumbled for the phone. The woman, a casting assistant at Paramount, was calling to say the director would like to hear her read. For a moment Terry thought it was a joke. Who would do this? She couldn't imagine. She'd sent off an audition tape months ago. The woman's voice, calm and impersonal, instructed Terry to pick up a script at an office in midtown. Terry scrabbled for something to write on and finally grabbed a Chinese take-out menu; water dripping from her hair smudged the ink and she had to ask the woman to repeat everything twice. When Terry hung up the phone, her apartment looked unfamiliar for a moment. It's only a callback, she told herself, wanting to quell the elation growing inside her. A part in a real movie. She saw herself in simple, elegant clothes, meeting with producers in high-rise offices instead of racing for the subway in a dress and heels, trying to avoid being splashed with slush. She would be plucked from the crowd. She thought of all those cattle call auditions, competing with several hundred other women, trying not to arrive flushed, out of breath because the train had been delayed or she couldn't find the address, then cramming into a dirty bathroom to fix her hair or her makeup, trying not to poke the woman next to her with her elbow and create any more competitive hostility than they already felt. When she called work to get out of her shift, Richie fired her. And this is what she has come to: standing in the street, listening to her own voice on her answering machine.

Climbing back up the stairs, she moved through the layered cooking smells that mingled on each landing: garlic on the second floor, something that smelled like cabbage on the third. She felt foolish for walking all the way down to check. Inside, she avoided looking for the light on her machine. Why didn't they call? Too ethnic looking? It had been said before. She resembled her mother's family, all from southern Italy with dark hair and olive skin. These days she didn't bother to audition when they wanted an all-American type. Growing up, she wouldn't have known what ethnic meant; in Brooklyn, everyone came from somewhere. When she went to college upstate, she learned that there were WASPs, and other Americans were defined by their difference from the fair-haired norm: Italian American, African American, Irish American, Native American. When she started trying out for plays, she learned to accept being labeled as Mediterranean, just as she accepted that she was young and pretty. She could not accept her accent. At the movies, on television, she had learned what her voice implied—gum chewing, decaled fingernails, leopard-skin collar on the winter coat. By her sophomore year in college, she had smoothed her Brooklyn accent into a voice that was educated, unplaceable. She had set out to lose it in high school, knowing, even then, that her voice would always place her as a girl from Brooklyn. She spent hours in front of her bedroom mirror, watching her mouth as she tried to reshape its sounds: *new yawk, new yaawk*; she hated the mean-sounding vowels that inevitably formed in her mouth. She wanted to say "York," elegant and round, British-sounding, opening her mouth so the sound would become tall, spacious, the roof of her mouth a cathedral: *yawk, yaawk, yerk, york, York*. She'd never do Shakespeare if she sounded like the voices at home.

She flopped onto her open bed and kicked the Help Wanted section onto the floor. January was a lousy month to look for work. She walked over to the stack of Day-Glo plastic crates that served as her closet and pulled out the pieces of her job-hunting uniform: short skirt, black stockings, heels.

Out in the street, people were brightly wrapped against the

cold. Everyone seemed to be carrying something: a hatless woman struggled down the street with a leafy houseplant, its greenness surprising in the gray air. Two clean-cut young men came out of the Erotic Baker, the smaller man carrying a white pastry box. She tried to imagine what was in the box, who they were bringing it to. She studied how people moved, how they walked and carried their shoulders, the various ways they negotiated the puddled curbs. Going to read for the director she'd felt purposeful, as if something large was being set in motion. She would look back and be able to pinpoint it—the part that changed everything. And it had happened just as she was beginning to lose faith. Studying acting was a filter through which she viewed her life: every feeling and reaction could be studied and used in the building of a character. The economy of using her life in this way pleased her, as if, and she knew this wasn't true, the living itself was not sufficient.

She walked down Columbus Avenue and inquired about jobs in any restaurant that looked promising. At Columbus and 74th, she walked under a bright awning that showed a man and a woman with cartoon balloons drawn above their mouths, "Italian? Argentine!" She walked in and asked the bartender about a waitressing job. He glanced at her, twisted a sheaf of cocktail napkins into a swirl, and set them on the bar.

"I'll buzz the manager. Her name is Marie."

The dining room had white stuccoed walls and a fireplace at the back. Two men sat at a table in the corner, a bottle of red wine between them, talking quietly. Terry picked up a menu lying on the bar. Expensive steaks, grilled meats—if the food was good she could make some real money. A short, round woman with silvery hair hurried up to the bartender, and ignoring Terry, dropped a thick sheaf of papers on the bar.

"Tommy, some of these tickets don't match. And we're missing a case of Concha y Toro. The Cabernet Sauvignon."

She turned to Terry and looked her over without shaking her hand. Marie was a buxom woman, and in a bright, red blouse it was hard to tell where her breasts left off and the rest of her began. She asked Terry where she had worked, why she left. Terry didn't bother to lie.

"We need a pretty girl here. We had a girl, but she did too

much coke, and I fired her." Marie talked very fast, tapping her painted fingers on the bar. She reminded Terry of a yappy, overfed dog.

Marie led her down a hallway and into the back dining room. The late afternoon sun came through a skylight into a room that was unprepared, slightly dilapidated, like an unfinished set. Next to an espresso machine, a long table was covered with candles, stacks of red tablecloths, bales of linen napkins, and rows of cut-glass jars filled with unfamiliar sauces. A group of men sat at one end of another long table, talking and laughing over an afternoon meal. Marie poured herself a cup of coffee, said something in Spanish, and the men all turned to look at Terry. They nodded and smiled like a group of cousins at a wedding.

"Let me introduce you to Sergio, our chef." Marie waddled toward the kitchen and pushed through the swinging doors.

Sergio, a tall, thickset man in a white apron, greeted Terry by nodding in her direction. When he came forward to shake her hand, she saw his rhinestone earrings, large bright clusters set above studded strands of glass. Seeing Terry's gaze, he pursed his lips and patted his dark curly hair with his palm. Terry grinned.

"Sergio is temperamental, but he's a wonderful chef," Marie said. She patted his hairy arm, speaking as if he wasn't there.

"I will try to be patient while you are learning, but I must warn you." Sergio put his hands on his hips and Terry thought of a football player imitating a schoolteacher. "When a plate is ready, it must *never* wait. Only for this will I yell at you."

"Let me go over the menu with you," Marie said. "There are probably some things you'll need to know. You'll need to learn some Spanish if you're going to make it here."

Terry never had problems making herself understood. In the past, when a busboy or dishwasher didn't speak much English, she would pantomime what she needed. She tried to think of it as another acting exercise. But Marie had not been kidding; none of the busboys spoke any English. Juan, who'd been assigned to her section, merely grinned at her requests.

"Excuse me, miss, could we have some more water?"

She heard Sergio's bell. Her order for another table was up.

"Yes, of course." She smiled and looked around for Juan. She found him smoking a cigarette by the espresso machine.

"Juan, I need some water on table five."

He grinned. She held up a sweating water pitcher and pointed to the table where the man was sitting with his back to them. "Agua," she said.

Juan frowned and took a sip from his coffee cup. As he carried the pitcher of water toward her tables, Terry heard Sergio's bell again. Swinging out of the kitchen, she saw, from the corner of her eye, that Juan had started with the closest table in her section and topped off the water in every glass. He was nowhere near the man who had asked for it.

"I'm sorry," she said. "I'll get the busboy right away."

She caught Juan's eye and nodded to the table where the man was waiting. Juan held up the empty pitcher triumphantly.

Terry served the food, got the water herself, then she crooked a finger at Juan and led him toward the back. "No tips. Can you understand that?" She looked straight at him, and his brown eyes grew large, surprised. A sullen expression thinned out his rosebud mouth. She knew he understood her, at least partially. "I'm not going to give you one fucking cent unless you take care of my tables the way you're supposed to." Her voice was quiet—she knew it was low to threaten such a thing. Even in anger, she was ashamed of her meanness.

One of the other busboys came up behind her. He said something quietly to Juan, who pouted and whisked the pitcher away.

"Juan, he is easier to make diplomacy with than push." The man's expression was grave, almost sorrowful. He had a round face with high cheekbones; in the dim light he looked almost Chinese. His hair was thick and straight, awkwardly cut into a helmetlike shape. The odd cut emphasized his features, which, looking more closely, she saw were not Asian at all. He had deep-set eyes, a slightly flattened nose. Although he wasn't old, forty at most, the shape of his features seemed Indian, somehow ancient. Terry found herself staring; she couldn't read his expression.

"I'm sure you're right." Terry set down the tray she was clutching. "But it's like he's doing it on purpose, to bait me."

"Bait you?" he looked puzzled.

"Bait. Catch, like a fish," Terry explained.

"Oh, I do not think he wants to catch you," the busboy said seriously.

"I don't mean he wanted to catch me," Terry giggled. "I know Juan's not interested. It's slang, sort of, for trying to trick someone, trying to make someone mad."

"I see." He closed his eyes for a moment, as if committing something to memory. "What would help, with Juan, is to learn a little Spanish."

Terry glanced over at her tables. Juan was walking up and down ostentatiously, belly pushed out like a small child, the water pitcher in his hand.

"My name is Alberto." He made a little bow.

"I'm Terry."

"Teresa," he said solemnly. And looking over his shoulder, "I must go to my tables."

Every day she waited for the call. It seemed that a judgment was being decided on the past ten years of her life. If she got the part, it meant that her persistence and hard work had paid off. And if she didn't? Did it mean that she'd been fooling herself? Hoping for something she didn't have the talent for? She'd seen a movie the other night about a basketball player who couldn't keep from gambling on himself. In different places she thought the movie was about to end, and it occurred to her, as she sat in the darkened theater, that wherever the story ended determined what you thought about the character. If it ended when he was on a streak, then his bet had been worth it. If it ended when he was down, it meant he'd risked too much, one too many times. For her it was all one long gamble. She was thirty-two years old. She'd worked fairly consistently, more than a lot of people, but all the productions were in downtown performance spaces, off-off-off Broadway. She knew she was a better actress than she was ten years ago, but she had nothing to show for it except a mediocre résumé and portfolio of head shots that made her look more glamorous than she was. When she wasn't acting, it was easy to tell herself that she was only a hopeful waitress, nothing more. She remembered coming home from college and telling her parents she'd be waitressing instead of getting a regular job.

"Four years of college and you want to wait tables?" her mother had said.

"Ma, I majored in drama. The whole idea of waitressing is so that when I get an acting job I can work around it."

"Why don't you teach? It's steady, good money. You go to college and become a waitress?"

Her father had watched them, faced off against each other, and when her mother turned to him to take her side, he would only smile. So they had relented, years ago, and her mother accepted her eldest daughter's floating life as a kind of transitory burden that would one day be laid to rest.

She had waited tables all over Manhattan, mostly with aspiring actors and actresses, hopeful writers and singers, all of them believing that their real lives lay elsewhere, all of them knowing how few of them would make it. There was an unspoken belief that the way their lives turned out would not only be a matter of talent and hard work, but finally there would be a deciding measure of luck or fate. And of course it was impossible to know how your luck would turn out unless you played to the end of your hand. This hadn't scared her when she was younger, but lately she had started to think that if success was not her fate, then it meant she was sacrificing a life of comfort and security for sleeping on a foldout sofa, living in an apartment where the shower was in the kitchen, and what would remain, at the end of it all, would either be a romanticization of her past or an acknowledgment of its insignificance.

This waitressing job seemed different because most of the waiters and busboys had found at least part of what they wanted: they had made it to New York. Of course, once they arrived it wasn't easy. Many of the busboys were men, older than her. They lived in large numbers in small apartments in Queens; they worked several jobs to send money home.

One afternoon, after a hectic lunch and a small take on tips, she tapped Alberto on the arm.

"I've been thinking about what you said. I'd like to learn some Spanish."

"And you would teach some English also?"

He was so earnest. She studied him in the afternoon light, the fine wrinkles around his eyes, his tie still done up.

"You come to work one hour early tomorrow?" he asked.

"Well," she was surprised by his seriousness, "okay."

When she arrived at ten o'clock the following morning, Alberto was waiting, drinking a cup of coffee and looking at the *New York Times*. When he saw her come in, he got up to pour her coffee.

"Isn't the *New York Times* kind of hard to read?" she asked.

"I read better than talk," he said. "I study English in school, many years ago. Also, I think it is important to read the right paper, yes?"

"Well, I guess. The *Post* isn't exactly a class act."

He smiled, and she sensed that she had missed the point.

"In my country, it is important to read the right papers, to know what they are saying, but it is a mistake to rely on them. You can't always read in public like here."

"Where are you from?" she asked.

"Paraguay."

"What did you do there?"

"Dentist."

"You were a dentist? Why did you leave?"

Alberto put his hands together in front of his lips, then opened his hands in a gesture as if to say, *who knows*?

"It is a dangerous place to live," he said finally.

"Do you have family there?"

"All. My wife. Three children. I could not bring them now, but I am sending money home. You like to see?" He pulled out his wallet and opened it to a photo carefully covered in plastic. Terry looked at a woman with dark hair piled above a round, pretty face. Her fingernails were polished; gold glittered at her wrist. Her plump, graceful arms encircled three children: two boys, and a little girl in a frilly pink dress. The boys were smiling, one grinning broadly; the little girl was serious. She had Alberto's eyes. He ran his fingertip around the picture, then pointed to each and told Terry their names. She imagined him alone, holding the small, covered photo in both hands, lifting it to his lips as a priest would kiss a Bible.

"They're beautiful. All of them," she said.

"I miss them very much."

"Were you political there?" she asked.

"No."

She took a sip of coffee, feeling she had intruded.

"I need to learn good English so I can become a waiter. It is the most important thing for me—to get them out," Alberto said.

He had brought a small pad with him, and she watched his hands, deft and dark, as he wrote out simple verbs in neat handwriting. On his right hand, a small scar curved along the flesh between his thumb and his first finger. It looked like something from a childhood mishap, a soft, light crescent in his skin. She made a list of what she wanted to say: "I need a fork on table five." Alberto wrote: "Yo necessito un tenedor a la mesa cinco, por favor."

On the way home, she strolled up Columbus Avenue. It was warm for January, and she bought the *New York Times* and sat down on a bench near the planetarium. She started to read an article on the front page, but after two paragraphs, she was confused. Funding for the Contras, Sandinistas, FMLN; the news was a mysterious conversation she was too late to catch up on. At least she knew that Paraguay was in South America, somewhere near Brazil. She knew that Central and South America were totally different, but they seemed tied together. Or maybe it was just her perspective. She thought of that poster of New York that showed Manhattan as the center of the earth: everything beyond New York was spread out and small, foreign countries merely flattened mounds on the landscape. She pushed the paper into an overflowing garbage basket.

Down the block, next to the planetarium, a group of schoolchildren was getting off a bus. Each child paused before jumping off the last step; a curly-haired woman in a slicker held their arms as they hopped down. The children milled around on the cobbled sidewalk; the few who wore bright rubber boots marched fearlessly through the slush; others picked their way around the cobbled puddles. Her parents had brought her to the planetarium when she was small. She remembered thinking that the chairs were like church; when she leaned against the back, her knees didn't meet the edge and her feet stuck out. She had rubbed her hand back and forth against the upholstery nap, feeling the small resistance that could be pushed just so far before it bent the other way. And she remembered, so clearly, the deep, baritone voice of the man who explained the galaxies and the way the planets and stars were made. The lights went out, his voice boomed out of the ceiling above her, and somehow she was spinning back to the beginning of time, before dinosaurs even, and then—she fell asleep. It became a family joke, how much she'd looked forward to going, then fell asleep. She had begged her parents to take her back. She was sure she had missed something important, a kind of necessary secret, and when she fell asleep the second time, and woke to find her mother rubbing her arm and the yellow lights coming back up, she had cried so hard that her father had to carry her back to the car. Of course they thought she was crying because she had missed the lights, the stars, but what she couldn't explain was that she cried because, once again, she had missed the large voice that explained how everything worked. She sensed that in this unraveling of Earth's beginning there was a secret, some clue to looking forward and understanding what the future held. Her newspaper started to fly out of the garbage bin, and she stuffed it back down. Has she been asleep without knowing it? She had persisted, and worked hard, because it seemed that everything was possible, eventually she would make it. Had she missed what the voice might have said? She wrapped her coat around her and got up from the bench.

No one called about the part. Every morning, it was her first waking thought. Some days she tried to forget it; on others, she checked her phone machine every hour. She wished she had someone to talk to. She didn't tell anyone in her family because one person would surely tell another and she didn't want to raise their hopes. Karen was gone. She touched a photo crookedly tacked to her kitchen cupboard, a picture of her and Karen, their sophomore year at college. They had studied acting at Syracuse and moved to New York together. Karen was so much her physical opposite, blond and petite, that they rarely auditioned for the same parts. They both knew this was a factor in their long friendship. Last year, after a long streak without work, Karen had gotten a toothpaste commercial. Then one evening, when they were sitting at home, drinking a bottle of wine, Karen's agent called to say she was on the shortlist for a commercial for some kind of new sanitary napkin, something with wings. *With wings!* They had laughed hysterically, and in the midst of their laughter, Karen sat up very straight and looked at Terry. "I've spent ten years working at this and my career is going to consist of toothpaste and Kotex commercials?" Neither of them knew what to say. A few months later, Karen met a Venezuelan businessman at one of her waitressing jobs and she simply left—got married and moved to Caracas. She'd left Terry a long letter with a check written on her fiancé's account for an amount far exceeding several months' rent. Aside from the loss of her friendship, Karen's defection had set up a corrosive sense of doubt. Terry tapped the photo by its corner and spun it around on the tack. Roulette. This was all a crapshoot. She was almost glad to go to work that night.

After the shift, she and Sergio sat over a carafe of red wine and she told him about her audition.

"So the fact that I haven't heard from them is driving me crazy. Sometimes I think they don't want me. Sometimes I think they need to cast other people before they tell me yes, or maybe they have to see me read with someone. It could mean they're having production problems; it could mean they don't want me." She always circled back to this.

"Oh! A movie!" Sergio's hands fluttered around his mouth. "How long has it been since you read for the big man?"

"Three weeks."

"That is not long."

She knew he was right. She was too impatient. She wished she could think about something else.

"Where are you from, Sergio?"

"Peru."

"Why did you leave?"

"A queen like me?" Sergio laughed. "I would not be tolerated in the town I come from, and I tell you—" Sergio leaned forward, confiding. "I always knew I would come to New York, always." He patted her hand. "If you believe you are meant to be in the movies, then you will get your part." He poured her a glass of wine. "You should have your numbers done."

When Marie was satisfied with Terry, she let her work dinners, which were harder work but better money. At night the back dining room looked wholly different: tiny lights on ficus trees placed strategically around the room reflected up into the large skylight like a thick net of stars. Spanish music played quietly in the background. She charmed a fresh audience of customers each night; some of them flirted with her, and she smiled lightly, promising them nothing without being too standoffish and jeopardizing her tip.

When Alberto was assigned to work with her, everything flowed more smoothly. Silent and efficient, he orbited her gracefully; he watched the tables without hovering, took care of things before she asked. He smelled of something soft and unfamiliar, not cologne, but soap maybe, sandalwood. She watched him from a distance as the shift slowed down. A dentist. Could his family imagine what his life was like? She imagined him sitting in his apartment at night, writing his letters home.

Sometimes she thought about him at night, before sleep. He had a wife, a whole family, *stop thinking,* she told herself. It seemed she'd been telling herself this for weeks now, about every aspect of her life—*stop thinking, don't imagine, don't want.* "You're just lonely." Out loud, it sounded melodramatic. "All you want is a distraction," she whispered to herself. She fell asleep and dreamed of visiting Alberto at his home in Paraguay. Everything was white. Stone-white road leading to his house, white stucco walls. Lots of bright flowers. His wife was gracious, but she studied Terry silently. She knew that something had happened. Terry woke from her dream feeling guilty. Nothing's happened, she told herself. Nothing.

Several mornings a week she met Alberto in the sunny back room. He was always there first, shirt pressed, tie done up. She wrote out the sentences for what she needed to learn: "Table eight needs soup spoons. These are not the right glasses for red wine." Alberto took the piece of paper and wrote the sentences in Spanish underneath. His hands were long and slender; they didn't match the broad curves of his face.

"Does it take a lot of money to get them out?" she asked.

"There are other problems than money."

"Will you have trouble with papers, green cards?"

"Yes."

She picked at the edge of the paper he had written on.

"Nothing is safe. Even if you are very careful. No political. Fear, carefulness, these do not protect you in my country."

She looked at him for a long moment. She wanted to touch his hand, to run her finger along the soft crescent scar. She moved her hands in her lap. She wanted to say something comforting, to offer some small article of faith, but any sureness she might offer would be a platitude, and false.

"Has anything happened to people that you know—at home, I mean?"

"Yes."

One of the other waiters heard her question and said something in Portuguese. Alberto shook his head.

"You should tell her about that. Learn those words," the waiter prompted.

"There are some things that should not be translated," Alberto said.

"What?" Terry asked.

"There are things I do not want the words for in any other language." Alberto took his pad and closed it. "It's time to go to work."

Lunch that day was hectic, but even in the rush, she checked her answering machine twice. She had the feeling that someone was trying to get in touch with her, but each time she called, her own voice answered. Maybe they're deciding now, she thought. Maybe they're choosing me this minute.

After the shift, Sergio made a hot meal for the staff. For the busboys, she guessed it was their biggest meal of the day. Sergio, because Marie decreed it, usually served a cheap cut of meat and some rice, as well as whatever vegetable soup was left over from lunch. Terry made herself salad. That afternoon, Marie noticed the dishwasher eating a cup of seafood chowder and she stormed into the kitchen to yell at Sergio, who marched her right back out the swinging doors.

"One cup left! One cup! You want I should save it for dinner? It's for this little one here." Sergio loomed over the dishwasher and smoothed his hair like a woman soothing a small pet. "You will have no chef for dinner if you don't get off my back, Marie!" Sergio's voice rose to a shriek and he swept into the kitchen. Marie hurried after him. Alberto looked up at Terry and smiled.

When she was done eating, Terry asked the bartender for a glass of red wine and sat down at a separate table to count her tips. Alberto sat at the end of a long table with the others. When he tipped back in his chair, his shirt pulled open at the collar and she saw the long scar, the soft skin like a crooked pink finger, running from the corner of his jaw, down the side of his neck. She felt her throat go tight, her fingers tremble. She closed her fingers around the stem of her glass. Alberto set the front feet of his chair back down on the ground and gently pulled his collar closed. He tightened his tie.

The next afternoon Terry walked into the restaurant and saw Marie sitting at a table with a man Terry didn't recognize. Terry waved, but Marie didn't acknowledge her. The bartender looked more surly than usual.

"Hey, Tom." She leaned over the bar and whispered. "What's up?"

"There's money missing from the lunch shift on Monday and Marie is pissed off. Everyone who worked that day has to take a lie detector test," he said.

Terry snorted. In back, no one was talking about it. Sergio kissed her on the cheek and asked her to write the specials on the board. Alberto walked over and touched her arm.

"You heard?"

"Tom told me," she said.

"This is trouble," Alberto said slowly. "Missing money is no good."

That night, a small sign posted in the kitchen listed the employees who would have to take a lie detector test. The list included everyone who worked on Monday. Juan studied it and made a disdainful spitting sound.

"Marie is a pig," he said. "All that coca and still so fat. Miss Piggy." Juan pressed his finger up against the bottom of his nose. Terry couldn't help but laugh.

When she arrived to set up for lunch the next day, Juan wasn't there. Friday lunch was always the busiest shift, and by twelve thirty, everyone was frantic. Water glasses went unfilled, tables were left uncleared; even Alberto couldn't keep up. One customer stiffed her badly. Every time she skidded into the kitchen, she wished she could transform the dishwasher into a busboy.

After the shift, they all settled down to eat. Sergio had made a pot of stew, something to soothe them. The dishwasher started to tell a story, something about his mother, but he was speaking too quickly for Terry to follow. Sergio pinched his cheek. The bartender ran into the room.

"Immigration!"

Everyone jumped from his chair. Sergio ran for the kitchen, the others for the Columbus Avenue exit. Three men in suits ran into the room just as the last pant leg flickered out the door. They shoved past Terry, dodging the fallen chairs, running out into the street. Terry grabbed her purse and ran after them. Pushing through the heavy door, she heard a screech of brakes. The sharpness of the sound seemed to ruffle the awning above her head. She blinked in the sunlight. There was no trace of the waiters' black and whites, and for a moment she felt deserted. Then she saw a motionless car on the other side of the street. She felt a pulse in her throat; she tried to swallow, but couldn't. The light changed and a stream of cars blocked her view. A loud buzzing filled her head. The traffic kept her from getting across, and finally she waded out into it, stepping up onto the bumper of a gridlocked taxi. The driver appeared to be shouting, but she only saw his angry mouth; she couldn't hear him through the glass. On the other side of the street, she pushed through a small crowd. Alberto was lying by the curb, his compact body bent at an odd angle, his left leg flung out in a grotesque sideways kick.

She knelt beside him. His head was twisted to one side and blood seeped out of his mouth. His tie was still done up. His eyes, slightly open, showed only white. She heard herself yelling for a doctor, but her voice was being sucked back inside her, her words no louder than a whisper.

She felt someone behind her, hands on her shoulders, a beard by her ear.

"There's no point in a doctor, there's nothing to do." It was the bartender; his voice was quiet. He pulled her by the shoulders, led her out through the small crowd.

She couldn't go back into the restaurant; she started to walk up Columbus Avenue. Behind her, the sound of an ambulance sang, *late, too late,* but the siren's increasing loudness seemed small, inconsequential.

She passed restaurants and bars, passed the street where the planetarium sat at the edge of Central Park, and she thought of her childhood desire for that all-knowing voice, her fear that she had missed something she needed to know. She remembered the afternoon when Alberto talked about getting his family out, how she'd been unable to offer him any reassurance; his life had seemed so small against everything he faced. And suddenly she felt an overwhelming sense of randomness, as if the invisible linkages of cause and effect seemed to float apart, dissipate, and she saw the people moving around her in the street, in the restaurants and cafés, were not protected, or overseen, but tenuously connected—unblessed, but also unfettered. And in the swirl of randomness, she felt an odd sense of lightness and clarity, as if in this vast disorder anything might be possible. Over the past weeks she had compared her difficulties with Alberto's, and had known that hers were trivial, but she saw it didn't matter; it was necessary to keep going. In the end it was like that movie with the false endings, or the undulations of a long, long story—everything depended on where you left off. She would keep waiting for the call, keep auditioning, and in the end, the story she would tell herself would be one that would reconcile her with her eventual success or failure. Everything around her stood out in high relief. She looked up at the high windows with their stone decorations on the buildings above her, the bare gray branches rising beyond the wall around the park, and the dome of the planetarium, which held those bright calculations of light, a story of contraction and expansion, and the delicate projections of how the turning world had come to be.

The Narrow Gate

This time she remembers the whole weekend. His hand against her forehead while she sucked, carefully, on the pipe, his fingers holding back her hair so it wouldn't catch fire. She concentrated on the rock. Delicate suck. Not like smoking pot. You had to go slow, not hit it too hard. His hand in her hair. *Breathe out, just a little.* Then an inhale, a deep breath of plain air. *Breathe out now, easy.* And she pursed her lips and exhaled slowly, emptying herself, and as she reached the bottom of her breath her eyes closed and the darkened room swirled into a silver bloom behind her eyelids and everything went away. She was standing in the kitchen, but she felt as if she'd been tipped backward, off her feet, tipped a little sideways and spinning out into the darkness. She inhaled slowly, held until her chest grew tight, anticipating the long, sliding exhale into clarity. The pattern that filled the weekend. She sits up, startled. She is breathing like that here. The man across from her doesn't notice. He's reading a book. Something's clenched too tightly in her hand. Clipboard. God, she actually came here. She will stop. Stop while he's gone. A few weeks, at least. He is off taking pictures. She sees his photos in magazines: Germany when the wall came down, Russian victims of radiation experiments, AIDS babies, the Rumanian baby market, people selling kids for TVs, a VCR. Unbelievable. Surfaces reveal the core. She closes her eyes. No one would think of her coming here. The woman who founded the place was some kind of Chinese Mother Theresa. Acupuncture to quit. Long article in the paper. Free if you couldn't pay.

The form on the clipboard begins with simple questions: name, address—but Marthe feels hot and confused, unsure of what to write. She'll put down some other name. No one will ever know. *Put a check mark next to the drugs you use daily. Put an X next to drugs you use once to several times per week: Alcohol, Cocaine, Crack, Pot, LSD, Dilaudid, Speed, PCP, Codeine, Heroin, Demerol, Percodan, Percocet, Darvon, Lomotil, Talwain, Quaaludes, Nembutal, Seconal, Phenobarbital, sleeping pills or other depressants, Methedrine, Exstacy, Ice. Have you ever been in a methadone maintenance program? When did you conclude that methadone was not a good therapy for you?*

Some of the drugs she's never even heard of. Carefully she checks off alcohol, pot, sleeping pills. Her pencil hovers over the soft blue words. Mimeograph. Nobody uses mimeograph machines anymore. The form reminds her of quizzes in high school, unfamiliar words in soft, blue type, waiting to be defined: *Ethnocentric, Anthropomorphic, Treaty of Versailles.* The newspaper article called this place a community clinic: grassroots, no government funding; women with children came here so the city couldn't trace them and put their kids in foster care. Acupuncture stopped the cravings—you could just get a treatment, you didn't have to stay. She had saved the article for weeks. She recognized the address: south of Mount Pleasant, at the edge of the Adams Morgan gentrification. She wouldn't run into anyone she knew.

As soon as she walked in the door, she wanted to run out, say she must have the wrong address, but the woman at the desk looked up.

"You've never been here before, is that right?" she asked.

Marthe nodded. She couldn't speak until she sat down in the chair next to the desk. She remembered going for a pregnancy test her freshman year at college; she didn't want to say, out loud, why she was there.

She stares down at the clipboard. *How long have you been using? Have you had periods of abstinence during this time?* She tries to guess at the right answer. Abstinence. Christmas, maybe, when she went to see her parents. Drinking didn't count. Of course she'd taken some Valium with her, maybe a few lines for the drive home.

She puts down Marthe Kongsburg, which is not her last name, and gives a fake address in Northwest D.C. They don't have to know. The clinic reminds her of an advocacy office—broad-leafed plants and posters only partially hide the chipping paint. Everything seems worn by use and cleaning. She leans back in the armchair and looks up. Patches of ceiling tiles are stained by water, a dried amber discoloration over the perforated tiles. Under her feet the mustard-color carpet is thinned, dark in odd places, as if it had been worn down in some other pattern of human traffic and then transported here. The waiting room contains three dilapidated armchairs and a few old wooden school chairs with desks attached to their arms. She had chosen the armchair that seemed cleanest, and sitting down, she sank low to the ground. Across the room, a young man with dreadlocks has a baby on his lap. When he looks up, sees her staring, he nods at her, then shifts the baby onto his shoulder and goes back to studying a thick textbook.

She is supposed to bring the clipboard back to the reception area. She stands up and automatically reaches for the doorjamb. Everything will go black for a moment. She keeps her head upright so it won't be too obvious. The woman is explaining something about Medicaid to a person on the phone. She talks slowly, explaining why the codes won't work for acupuncture. She nods for Marthe to sit down. The woman's face is dark, unlined, framed by soft curly hair; the whites of her eyes are thickened, slightly yellow. A long beaded earring hangs from one ear. Her other earlobe is split where an earring would have hung. Marthe startles when she notices it, tries not to flinch. Medicaid. She doesn't belong here. Her seat bones feel hard and sharp against the chair. She wishes the woman would get off the phone and talk to her. She wants to snatch the forms back, change her answers, change her name; instead, she gets up slowly and goes back to the waiting room. She looks up at the smudged ceiling, then closes her eyes. Needles. They're supposed to use disposable needles. They better. Wouldn't it be her luck if she got AIDS from trying to quit?

She stares at the man across from her as he studies his book. Is he a patient, or is he waiting for someone? The child is sleeping now. Boy or girl? She can't tell. Tiny mouth half open, tiny fists, tiny sneakers. She slides down in the armchair and closes her eyes.

She wanted to. It's not his fault. He just showed her how. His hand in her hair as he lit the pipe, told her not to breathe too hard. They were still pretending to be just friends. She remembers the exact moment everything turned, became charged. She had run into him on the street after he'd been away for several weeks, and she'd said something about how it was nice to know he was back in the city. He said it was nice to be missed. He didn't look at her when he said it. His voice was serious, unflirtatious. She stared down at the sidewalk, noticed the grass growing up between the cracks. Such a simple start. They had only two friends in common, but they kept running into each other. They don't fit into each other's lives. She thinks his clever, more up-and-coming friends are pretentious, perhaps smart, but not really intelligent. She doesn't like his apartment or the art he buys. Expensively nihilistic, she once told him. And of course she isn't cynical enough for him. She's too sincere, too eager. He's away for weeks at a time. He calls her from other countries, and the occasional lags in the line, the subterranean or atmospheric delays, only point out how unsustainable they would be in the outside world. They've come to know each other too well. So they sleep with other people. Even the idea of each other is too much.

Her scalp tingles. The heat in her throat spreads down into her stomach. She wishes there was something to read here. On the opposite wall, a poster shows the human body with muscles and organ systems drawn in detail. The picture reminds her of a childhood encyclopaedia with overlapping transparencies of the human body systems. On the poster, the lines run up and down the body with little points along the lines, "The Meridians," it says. Another chart shows a large, flesh-colored picture of the outer ear. Each tiny point on the ear shows the organ that point affects—a tiny heart, lungs, stomach, and eye, others are harder to guess. What does a liver look like? Ugly, brown. A spleen? At the back of the room, behind a counter, shelves are filled with brightly colored boxes and bottles, all labeled in Chinese.

A Chinese man wearing gold spectacles and a blue Mao jacket comes around the doorway and nods to her. "Marthe?" he asks. She follows him down a narrow hall and he leads her into a small room containing two chairs and a doctor's table covered with paper.

"Please sit down. Take off your watch," he says.

She removes it, and the damp, round mark on her arm reminds her that she didn't shower that morning. She remembers how she felt when she first woke up. Fried. Her brain somehow stuck in first gear. She had a sudden moment of terrible fear, that she might stay like that forever, everything fuzzily simplified to necessity: thirst, aspirin, as if she'd lost the capacity for thought. It didn't feel like morning, just a continuum of light and dark, a sense of dislocation, as if everything around her was in the wrong place, but she couldn't remember how it used to be.

He sits next to her in a chair, takes her hand, and places his first three fingers on the soft whiteness of her inner wrist. He closes his eyes. She feels his three fingers distinctly; the first finger pressing lightly, then the second, the third. With his eyes closed, his face is ancient looking; even with shallow circles under his eyes, he seems unreal. A statue listening to her pulse. She wants to ask what he's doing, but he silently lets go of one wrist and takes her other hand. The room is still. Through her pulse he seems to be listening to something very faint and faraway. Outside, she hears the scrape of the iron gate as it rings on the cement, letting someone in.

"Stick out your tongue." He examines her tongue for what seems to be a long time, then nods.

"Why did you feel my wrist?"

"I was taking your pulses. They tell me about your internal organs." His voice is quiet, unrevealing.

She feels nervous, petulant. She wants him to talk, to say something soothing.

"What do they tell you?" she asks.

He studies the clipboard for a moment without answering.

"You didn't mark crack, or coke, on here—that's what they tell me. Please, take off your shoes, lie down on the table."

She bends to hide her face while she fumbles with her shoes. How could he know from her pulse?

"You use disposable needles, don't you?"

"Yes." He holds up a fine needle, encased in plastic, to show her.

She lies down on the table and he pushes her hair back from her face. A cool swab of alcohol at the top of her ear. She presses her palms against the table, bracing herself. A small prick on the outside of her ear, then another, and another. She breathes out when he puts the needles in. Each time there is a tiny pinch, nothing more. She feels the alcohol on the tops of her feet. He puts one needle on the top of each bare foot. Then he bends each of her arms and sets them on her stomach. On each hand he pushes a needle into the flesh between her thumb and her first finger. She feels a charge, and then a dull ache.

"Ouch."

He rotates the needle in her left hand.

"It aches a little?"

"Yes."

"It's a strong point. Don't worry. These are all very shallow insertions. If either of these still hurts in a few minutes, I'll change them. I'm going to leave you here for a half hour or so. You may fall asleep. It would be good for you. You don't have to be anywhere, do you?"

"No."

"Good. We'll have a little talk when you wake up."

As soon as he shuts the door she picks up her head to look at the needles in the tops of her feet. So slender she can barely see them. On her hands she can see they aren't in her deeply; they tip away from her fingers like delicate antennae. She closes her eyes and breathes deeply. This will let her stop. He knows she lied.

Knows by her pulse. Unbelievable. She is tired of lying, excuses for being late, excuses for the blackouts that happen almost every night now. Alzheimer's Lite, she sometimes jokes, a line that always gets a laugh, distracting people from the fact that a whole piece of a night or day has eluded her. She has developed subtle ways of prompting, of routing a conversation so she can figure out how she got home, or where she'd been over the course of a long weekend. She will stop. It will all stop. She tries to relax and let her body ease. She closes her eyes. What a strange place this is, that she should come here. Her body doesn't feel any different. What if this doesn't work? Something has to. She just needs a breather, a little help slowing down. Her job doesn't help. She freelances: mostly radio voice-overs and commercials. The latitude of her schedule gives her too much time to get in trouble. He likes her voice. Men always do. Even as a child her mother coached her: your voice can be your most attractive feature. Modulation is important. Men don't like a grating voice. Right out of the fifties, her mother. Sally, Dick, and Jane. Talking, talking, talking, always the pull between them was there. He sees what she can become. He sees what others don't recognize, or don't articulate: *You still think that beauty lies in restraint and poise. It's sexy, but it's just a front. There has to be a counterbalance.* He smiles and waits. Her resistance is understood, but he refuses to seduce her with any false assurances. He is determined to tease her into making the first move. *You're afraid to try what you want. You want something you can't even admit to yourself.* They are always at the brink. He says these things to her, and then he leaves. Quebec, Croatia, Ceauşescu, Russian entrepreneurs, a picture worth a thousand . . . she has to stop.

When she wakes up, the room seems darker, as if hours have passed. The gate outside rasps the pavement. Someone coming out or in. Formless music seeps in from another room. As she picks up her head to look at the needles, the doorknob turns and she lets her head down.

"Sleep well?" he asks.

"I think so."

She doesn't feel the needles coming out. He dabs her ears and feet with alcohol and says, "Sit up, slowly now."

She sits up on the bed and rubs the top of one foot with the other. He reaches down and hands her her shoes. The humility of the gesture surprises her. She stares at his hands and takes her shoes slowly. Her socks are crumpled inside.

"You will need to come back here again," he says. For the first time she notices his accent isn't Chinese or American, it's something different, vaguely European. "For you, getting to sleep at night will be the most difficult thing. Rita will give you some herbs that you can make into tea at night, but you must try to sleep without alcohol or any pills."

"Even the drugstore kind?"

He looks at her for a long moment; there is no reproof in his gaze, only a kind of waiting. She remembers why she came and feels vaguely ashamed.

"Anything," he says. Then after a pause, "Why did you come here?"

"I guess I just wanted to stop for a while, take it easy."

"Then what?"

"I don't know."

"This isn't what you think. It doesn't work like that."

"What do you mean?"

"You have to want to stop. If all you want is a break, we can't see you here. There are too many others who really want to quit."

She hadn't expected this bluntness. She feels a falling sensation, as if the entire day is sliding out from beneath her.

"How I feel is not good enough?"

"It's not a matter of good enough. It's just that you don't seem to understand what you're doing here. Did you come on your own?"

She nods.

"Then you know." He looks at her for a long moment.

In the half-lit room, she can't read his eyes behind his glasses, but as he stares at her and waits, she feels herself sliding, sliding. It's that obvious. People know. She feels hot, humiliated.

"The acupuncture will help to lessen your cravings. It will balance your body. You've been up for too long. The acupuncture helps with the physical withdrawal, but we also suggest patients go to NA or AA—or even go to church. It's up to you. You can see Rita on your way out to make another appointment." He leaves the door open behind him.

She sits still for a moment. She thought she could just get a few acupuncture treatments and quit. She hadn't wanted this to be personal, complicated. She wanted to do it alone. When she bends to tie her shoes, her hands feel thick and uncoordinated, as if her thumbs don't have the strength to press against her other fingers. She ties her laces with big loops like a child.

She walks slowly out to the front desk.

"Now, we want you back here real soon. You have a job?" Rita asks.

Marthe nods.

"Regular hours?"

"No."

"Good, it gets busy in here after work. We'll put you down for three o'clock tomorrow." Rita hands her a brochure. "This is a list of meetings in Washington. There are NA meetings on Wednesday and Thursday nights, right upstairs."

The phone rings and Rita answers it. Marthe stares at the pink brochure. The printing is awkward and crooked. Ugly. She came here on her own. That should be enough. She will do it herself. No one will know. She holds the smudgy list of meetings: AA, NA, no.

"Okay," Rita says, hanging up the phone. "I can see you don't like the idea of going to meetings. You can try and tough it out yourself, but girl, we talk to people straight here and I'm going to tell you that you aren't here 'cause you're sitting pretty."

Marthe picks herself up out of the chair. Her face feels hot, as if she's been slapped. She tries to snatch the herbs off the desk, but her body feels blurry, incapable of moving too quickly. Reaching for the herbs, she knocks them onto the floor.

She fumbles for her purse and pushes out, against the door. She has to use both hands. She leans her weight against the door and sees herself as Rita must see her: not even strong enough to open a heavy door, but angry, a bratty child. Rita leans back in her chair, elbows resting on the chair arms, waiting to see what will happen next.

Marthe leans her cheek against the door. "I'm sorry," she says.

Rita gets up and comes over to her. She smells of something unfamiliar, dusky and comforting. She places the packet of herbs in Marthe's hand. "Don't be sorry, just get yourself back here tomorrow."

Marthe nods. She wants to smile, but if she smiles, she's afraid she'll weep.

"Three o'clock tomorrow," Rita says.

When Marthe gets outside, the day is still bright. Very bright. She puts her hand on the iron gate and lifts the latch. She pulls on the gate, hearing its high metal scrape against the pavement, the scraping song of a narrow opening.

The Music Underneath

I worked for Charlotte Beresford for several weeks before she told me about some of the au pairs who had preceded me: the Finnish girl who had an affair with the pub owner and got pregnant, the Dutch girl who kept a bottle behind the window curtain, not realizing the diminishing contents of her bottle was visible from the courtyard outside the house. Charlotte told me these stories in an amused tone, and I wasn't sure if her telling me was a sign of trust or a warning.

I had flailed my way through several majors at college, a term at a music conservatory, and a brief stint as a musician in the Boston subway, when I was accepted as the student of a prominent violinist who lived in Oxford. Kato's acceptance letter seemed like a sign, a marker of turning toward a more orderly life. I managed for several months on a semester abroad program, but when the term was over, I wanted to continue my lessons. Working as an au pair seemed the cheapest way to stay in England; work permits were difficult to get with so many people on the dole. Thinking back, it seems funny that it was music that led me to Charlotte and Barrington, when so much of what I learned there had to do with silence.

I found Charlotte's advertisement for an au pair in a small market in Oxford. When I called on the phone, her accent was distinct and upper class, but her voice was warm, spilling over its edges. We arranged to meet at the train station the following Saturday.

Waiting at the station, I watched parents retrieve their sons from boarding school for the weekend. The boys huddled on the platform in navy blazers and short gray pants, swatting each other with their satchels until they spotted the car that had come for them. Some left their friends reluctantly, while others, thin legs below their shorts, hurried to their mothers to be enfolded in wool and perfume. On the phone Charlotte had said she had three children; I'd forgotten to ask their ages. I looked up the hill at the dark steeples and square towers set against the flat, pearl-colored sky, the constant gray like a sullen child who pouts and threatens tears.

A small white car pulled up, and a tall, thin woman with long auburn hair climbed out. She moved quickly and loosely, her walk made her seem younger than she was. She wore a jade-colored sweater, loose around her neck, and low boots with slender high heels. The sweater set off her bright hair and brown eyes. Her nose was pointed and delicate, her mouth too wide. She was pretty in a well-tended way; her nail polish matched her lipstick. I felt dowdy and unplanned. I was wearing the only skirt I'd brought with me, an act of deference on my part. My usual outfit was outlandishly American: a pair of overalls and sneakers, anything else seemed to require too great an effort.

Driving back to the house, she explained that they lived in Barrington, a small village outside Oxford. She talked about her family as if I were a friend she had not seen in a long time. Her husband, David, was in the Philippines on special diplomatic assignment. He used to be with the Foreign Service and they had recently returned from living in Delhi for two years. She said she found it difficult to live without servants now, then she looked over at me.

"Of course the girls who come to stay with us aren't servants. We want someone who'll be a part of the family while they're with us. We have fun—lots of parties and guests and visitors." She turned to smile at me, hinting at something exciting below the surface of things, something that could not be told yet. In the following weeks, I saw how Charlotte thrived on anticipation in an almost childlike fashion. She gave dinner parties with unexpected themes. We'd make invitations from cloth or exotic paper, and she'd waggle her long fingers and describe a potentially disastrous or intriguing seating arrangement. She also used her enthusiasm to be charming with men, describing an upcoming party or fete with expectation in her eyes. "The house is a lot of work to keep up and I just need to have *some* help. David doesn't understand it, but he's away so much. Of course India *is* very different. You can't live without servants. They go to market for you, cook, it's easy to get spoiled." She smiled at me, implying that if I were to marry an ambassador or attaché that I would come to the same conclusion.

She said that Helen was fifteen, mad about horses, and they kept a pony on a neighboring estate. Rupert was thirteen, going off to school and he didn't want to go. He wasn't old enough to understand how important the right schools were. He felt it was unfair he was being sent away just because he was a boy. Cary, Caroline really, was five, and well, precocious. After hesitating a moment Charlotte said,

"One thing I like to make very clear, I do not allow anyone to hit my children. Cary can be difficult, but if there's any punishment like that, I will take care of it."

I wondered how horrible Cary would be. In the following weeks I found she was slightly spoiled and very intelligent. She would store up a series of questions that she unloaded before bedtime. She annoyed Charlotte with questions also—who was on the telephone, where was she going—and I didn't understand Charlotte's annoyance at her persistence until I understood what she had to hide.

Barrington consisted of about twenty thatched-roof houses, Mr. Busby's grocery store, a church, and two pubs. We turned into a gravel driveway that swept around a small stone fountain. The massive stone house, covered with vines, overshadowed every other house in the village. Charlotte explained it had been the rectory of the church across the way.

As we pulled into the driveway, I had the premonition I would be immersed in something I didn't understand yet. On the phone I'd made it clear that I needed to practice. I was not here for the "experience" of living in a foreign country. But crunching into the gravel drive, I felt on the edge of something I couldn't name.

The phone was ringing as we walked in the door. Charlotte rushed off to answer it, leaving me in a large entrance hall filled with heavy oak furniture. Life-size portraits of someone's ancestors, set in thick ornate frames, rose up the wall of the wide stairway. After waiting for several minutes, I walked into a study off the main hall. The room was filled with small paintings and engravings. I stared at the tiny worlds they contained and tried to imagine living in as many countries as Charlotte had. I wondered how her life felt to her, if it seemed like a long series of compartments, separate, but somehow related, or if the different phases had grown into a netted accumulation, as if everything added up to where she was then.

Charlotte finally returned and we went into the garden to meet Helen and Cary. Helen had long brown hair, fair skin, and a slow smile. She was struggling with a bridle she had taken apart to clean for Pony Club inspection. I asked a few questions about her pony and she launched into an evaluation of his likes and dislikes, faults and strengths. She poked at bits of dried soap in a buckle as she talked.

Cary had tiny freckles and enormous blue eyes, her mother's eyes in another color. Her soft hair was a shade between brown and blond. She smiled at me shyly, already conscious of her charm, and reported that Rupert had gone off with a friend. Charlotte nodded absently and suggested we fix lunch.

Afterward she drove me back to the train station and offered me a job. She seemed surprised, and slightly relieved, by my quick acceptance. We agreed that David would pick me up at the train station two weeks from that day.

As the train rocked through the late afternoon, I suddenly felt I had been in England for a very long time. I don't mean that I was homesick; it had more to do with that drawn-out sense of time that is sometimes part of being in a foreign country. It felt strange to imagine that the other students would be going home, or traveling in Europe, while I might stay the same length of time once over again. The summer stretched in front of me.

When I arrived at the train station two weeks later, a man who looked like a Burberry advertisement was standing on the platform with a boy in his early teens. I recognized them by the way they stood, not talking to each other. David picked up my suitcase and Rupert asked if he could carry my violin. When he felt its lightness, he held it like a machine gun and made a staccato sound in his throat.

"Rupert, the sound effects are unnecessary." David spoke without raising his voice or even looking at Rupert.

Rupert looked over at me. I smiled behind his father's back. He grinned and carefully set my violin on the backseat.

On the ride to Barrington, David asked where I had been at school and where my parents were from. Rupert sat quietly in back staring out the window. I knew his father's small talk infuriated him. He was a thin boy with a round, childish face. He wore his hair cropped short, and torn black jeans. In the mirror, I saw him watch a group of girls hurry past the skinheads clustered around St. Giles. I thought how different David and Charlotte were, remembering how she had confided Rupert's unhappiness, and restlessly smoked a cigarette.

My schedule at the Beresfords was convenient for practicing, but it was several weeks before I understood how convenient it was for Charlotte too. Three afternoons a week she was a guide at Blenheim Palace, Winston Churchill's family estate. She always went off in a pretty dress and perfume, and returned with anecdotes about her tour group or the other people who worked at the palace. Her enthusiasm for the job didn't strike me as unusual. Later I felt foolish; I hadn't noticed how she fussed over her makeup and hair, how cheerfully she rushed around the kitchen making sure we had everything for dinner before she left the house.

As soon as we'd met, Charlotte talked to me as if I might understand her. It was a form of flattery I had not yet encountered, the kind that can only be dispensed by someone who knows or guesses they are admired. Until I met her, my close friends were students my own age. We felt adult, detached from our childhoods. We didn't yet see our parents as people much like ourselves. Charlotte spoke to me as if I understood the intricacies of running a household, of being a woman. Her inclusion elevated me to a world of exotic travels and lovers in distant places. Her sudden moods, or a half-finished sentence completed with a gesture, made me feel I was hearing a piece of music that was foreign and somehow familiar.

Charlotte and I did the cooking and housework together. She was usually running late, pulling pans and kettles out of cabinets, turning the burners on high. She moved in her kitchen the same way she did outside. She would brush by a pot on the stove or come close to spilling something, always missing by a hair. We usually had guests for dinner, and Charlotte insisted on hot plates, warm rolls, and linen napkins on the table. When I first arrived, I felt like I was in a frantic cartoon, but after a while, I got used to the slow afternoons of cooking and gossip, and the last-minute rush of putting dinner on the table. When a guest complimented Charlotte on an unusual dish or presentation, she would smile at me across the table, knowing I understood the mishap that had caused our culinary improvisation.

One afternoon, in the midst of cooking, the phone rang. Charlotte answered it, and told me she'd take the call in her study. When she came back, her mood had changed. She ripped the paper off the roast we were going to make for dinner, and dropped it in the pan with a thud. She began to talk about how difficult she found David's absences. I had guessed he would be leaving sometime soon, but I didn't know when.

"He expects me to handle everything by myself, but when he comes back, he wants to be in charge of everything again," Charlotte muttered. She pulled a cutting board toward her and grabbed an onion.

"Did he tell you just now, over the phone?" I asked. It seemed an abrupt announcement, even for David.

"No, that wasn't him," Charlotte said. She didn't look at me. Her eyes were red. I couldn't tell if it was the onion or tears. I dug a dark spot out of a potato. I wasn't sure what to say.

"I'll go get Cary from school," she said. "I could use the walk."

She dropped her apron on the counter and hurried out the door.

Charlotte's disclosures unsettled me; her life seemed so perfectly finished. I believe the same thought had occurred to her, but with a different inflection, that her life was perfect, and somehow concluded.

One Sunday we had a former ambassador and his wife for dinner, and then an Oxford don and his daughter for tea. As soon as we finished with one batch of guests, we had to prepare for another. That evening, Charlotte and I were quiet as we cleaned up. She handed me a washrag, and at the same time brushed my bangs out of my eyes.

"Your hair grows so fast, we'll have to go into Oxford this week. I'll bring you to the man who does my hair." She held her hand on my head for a moment and looked at me. She'd been talkative all day, now the animation had left her face. Her eyes looked large. She looked older.

David wandered into the kitchen.

"Sundays always seem like one long eat." He sighed and turned on the kettle. "The Ingrams are so boring. They both talk at the same time, across the table. I kept imagining how they'd look if we could turn the sound off."

"We invited them because they've had us for tea *twice*." Charlotte's voice was furious. She twisted the rag she held in her hands. "I'd prefer not to see them at all. You don't think about how much work it is for me to be bored by them."

David looked up, surprised. Charlotte threw the rag on the counter. It made a loud slap, and she stalked out of the room. David looked after her, then followed her out of the kitchen.

I'd never seen her so angry. As I cleared up, I thought about how little they spoke when they weren't entertaining. David talked about his garden, or politics, but I couldn't remember him ever making a personal comment. He would ask Harriet about her pony, or Rupert about school, but their answers seemed to evaporate before penetrating him. He never acted more than mildly affectionate toward Charlotte. His household revolved around him without engaging him at all, like something he had once set in motion that now had a life of its own.

Shortly after that night, David left for the Philippines again. In the evenings Charlotte and I sat on an overstuffed sofa in her study and talked late into the night. Sometimes Helen sat with us, absorbed in a book or flipping through a catalog of horsey things. She was quiet by nature, and relieved by my presence in a way; she wasn't old enough to be interested in her mother's fascinations. Charlotte asked about my life in Boston, and about my adventures in London before I came to them. I was flattered by her interest. She confessed that she didn't know what to think when she first met me—she wondered if Barrington would be too quiet for me. After Harriet went to bed, we talked about the children. She also asked me about menus, and who I thought we should invite for dinners. I was learning from her that much depended on how things were presented.

Charlotte also talked about South America and India. She told me about being single and living in New York. I imagined her laughing at cocktail parties, her shiny hair piled on her head, anticipating the unexpected. When she talked about those times, I felt I was on the verge of an extraordinary life. I would finish school and something wonderful would happen. This was part of Charlotte's allure: her sense of anticipation was infectious. Her smile made you feel that an adventure was hidden just around the corner.

Late one afternoon Rupert walked into my room. I was sitting in an armchair with music spread across my lap, marking bowings for a new sonata.

"Rupert! You might knock," I said. "I might have been changing or something."

"But you weren't."

My violin was set on top of the bureau and he ran his index finger along the outside curve.

"You can pick it up if you want."

"No."

He walked over to my window and looked out over the roofs of the village.

"Why didn't my mother go to Blenheim today?"

"She did."

"No, she didn't."

"I saw her off myself," I said.

"Well, I saw her in Oxford walking down the street with some man."

Rupert stood with his back to me. I felt a horrible tickle in my throat, something way down inside. I wanted to ask him how she looked, what the man was like.

"What were you doing in Oxford this afternoon?" I asked.

"Lennie's mother gave us a ride in."

"How did you get back?"

"She brought me back to the Noke turnoff and I caught a ride at the Two Swans."

"Rupert, you shouldn't have. Something might have happened."

"Who was my mother with this afternoon?"

"Rupy, I don't know." I stood up and beckoned him over. He walked toward me reluctantly. He was at the age of being small enough to be held, but embarrassed by obvious affection. I hugged him and talked into his hair. I was afraid to look him in the face.

"She might have been talking with one of the officers or trustees about business there."

"Tour guides don't do that," he said.

"Maybe she's getting promoted."

He stiffened and pulled away from me. Then he walked out of my room and gently closed the door behind him.

After that day, I began to notice little things—that Charlotte rarely talked about her job when David wasn't home, her disproportionate impatience when Cary wanted to answer the phone herself. I wondered about every phone call that Charlotte chose to take out of the room, and what grew to disturb me, even more than the possibility that she might have a lover, was the fact that she hadn't told me.

Early one afternoon when I was going upstairs to practice, Charlotte stopped me on the landing and said she was going to visit her brother Graham in London for the weekend. He was in town for a few days, and they needed some time to talk. She asked that if her parents called, to please not tell them she was seeing Graham. They'd be terribly hurt that he wasn't coming out to see them.

I nodded and said it was fine, but later in my room I wondered if she was really seeing her brother. It seemed strange that he didn't want to see her parents.

I was quiet that evening as we were fixing dinner.

"I hope you don't mind staying with the children all weekend. You can take a few days off next week if you like," Charlotte said.

"No, it's no problem at all."

Charlotte stopped what she was doing and came over to me. She looked directly at me and lowered her voice.

"It's a bit difficult about Graham and my parents. My brother is gay, and my parents have no idea at all. They always tease him about finding a wife, and he doesn't want to hear all that now. He has some things he wants to talk to me about."

Her voice was serious and confiding. I looked back at her face, those deep brown eyes and her pained half-smile. I wanted to believe her.

On Saturday afternoon the phone rang. I heard the static, the space between crackles, and then I heard David's voice, small and distinct on the other end of the line. He asked for Charlotte.

I told him she wasn't there, and the frail connection spared me the effort of excuses. He left his number and said she should call back.

"Is everything all right?" I asked.

"Yes, everything's fine. But please ask Charlotte to call."

When I hung up the phone I felt something hard and dark in the pit of my stomach. I dialed the number Charlotte had left, but there was no answer. I tried it all afternoon, and finally, around supper time, Charlotte answered the phone. Her *hello* was tentative.

"Charlotte, it's me. David called. He said everything's all right, but he wants you to call him."

"Did you tell him I was in London?"

"No, I just said you were out."

"Thank you." She sounded awkward, knowing her question revealed her anxiety. "I'll see you tomorrow evening. If David calls back and we've missed each other, please don't mention that I'm here."

When she returned the following evening, she said "thank you" and hugged me, then hurried out to the children. I stood in the kitchen door and watched the last of the long evening light. I reminded myself that she simply might not want David to know that she had left the children with me for the weekend. But it seemed there was so much more. To ask her openly if she had been with someone else was not my place. I wanted her to tell me. I stood looking into the deep green and fading blue, and wondered if this was how everything happened, unspoken, below the surface.

After her return, Charlotte acted the same as always. The following week, her parents came to visit, so we didn't have time for our evening talks. I tried to create a small distance between us, to show that it didn't matter whether she told me or not, but she would take me aside and ask my opinion, or confide some small worry, and my coolness dissolved. One evening, we took a walk through the fields outside Barrington. We'd had a long weekend of entertaining. The sullen sky made the fields a deeper green, and dark birds landed on random stone walls and became a part of them. As we rounded back into the village, I said that I hadn't been inside the pub yet, referring to one of my predecessors. She laughed and suggested we stop for a drink.

The pub was dark and warm. We sat back on the upholstered banquette and allowed ourselves to be served. Charlotte ordered a Pernod, and intrigued by the cloudy concoction, I had one too. The licorice taste spun on my tongue, and I still associate the numbing sweetness with that night.

She talked about missing David, but over the past weeks, I found that David seemed more tangible in his absence than his presence. Charlotte regarded his reserve with a mixture of frustration and fascination, as if his restraint were a barrier only she could cross. As we talked about David, Charlotte's mind turned to Rupert. She worried that sending him away to school would instill this guardedness in him also. She talked about the friends they had made in Brazil, how much she loved their spontaneity. After her second drink, Charlotte started to tell a story. She stopped for a moment, as if to change directions, and then went on to tell me that she'd had an affair with a Brazilian diplomat while they were living in São Paulo.

"I don't know how it started, really." Her voice was low, almost a monotone. She stretched her hands on the table in front of her and stared at them as if they weren't her own. "The men there are different. Everyone flirts. At first I didn't take him seriously." She looked off and squinted thoughtfully, as if trying to picture a room they had slept in, or trying to see his face. She bent to sip her drink and I stared at the tendon in her neck, imagined a dark finger touching her throat.

I waited for her to continue. Sitting in that darkened room, watching her, a whole world swam into focus. I felt as if I'd been handed a piece of red transparency, the kind that comes with a picture as a prize in a cereal box. When you look at the cardboard cartoon you see one picture, but looking through the colored plastic, a second picture is revealed.

"I never imagined myself doing such a thing—it seemed impossible, but I wondered if David really loved me, or if I just fit into his life the right way." She added water to our drinks and lit a cigarette. I watched the drinks turn a lighter shade of yellow. "Timing can be everything. You should know that for yourself." She looked at me, her brown eyes dark. The lines around her mouth were sharp. "I didn't know what David would do if he found out I'd been unfaithful. I finally realized what I was jeopardizing—my family, my whole life. I was scared, and I broke it off."

Her words sounded sad and familiar, as if she had repeated them to herself many times. I wondered how it felt to carry her story, if it was something bright to be nurtured, or if she regretted the safer course her life had taken. She took a long pull on a cigarette. We sat quietly for a moment, as if mourning something.

"I don't know why I'm telling you this now." She watched a man throwing darts in the corner. I knew there was more; it pulsed in what was still unsaid. I waited for her to go on. Her green eyeliner had washed into a soft smudge below her eyes. I took my finger and wiped at a blot on her cheek. Charlotte reached over and squeezed my hand, then held it for a moment, as if to reassure me.

Charlotte thought a weekend in London would be fun for Rupert and a little break for us. She wanted to spend some time with him. The girls could stay with her parents. She'd also promised him a leather jacket to cheer him up.

The following weekend, we went to stay in Graham's flat in Portobello. When we arrived on Friday night, Charlotte unpacked while Rupert and I looked at the autographed eight-by-ten glossies on the wall. Graham directed films and spent most of his time in Los Angeles. I was impressed by all the stars I recognized. I followed Rupert into a small study and looked at Graham's books while Rupert fumbled around in the desk.

"You shouldn't go through people's things." I told him.

"He wouldn't care. This is what I was looking for." Rupert pulled a small hookah out of a drawer.

"What do you plan to do with that?" I asked. I knew Rupert had never gotten high by the way he had asked me about it when I first came to them.

"What do you put in this?" he asked.

"Hash."

"What do you know about my uncle?" Rupert put the mouthpiece to his lips but did not blow or draw on it.

"That he's a director," I answered.

"My uncle has a boyfriend. No one will talk to me about it." Rupert placed the pipe back in the drawer and shut it.

On Saturday morning Charlotte was in the bathroom for a long time. When she came out, she apologized for holding us up and said that she didn't feel well, something she ate last night must have been bad.

I didn't give it any thought until she lingered in the bathroom again on Sunday morning. She emerged pale and quiet, saying she had been sick. Her eyes were red, she held her hands over her belly. I pictured her going to her job in a pretty dress, a bracelet sparkling on her wrist, anticipating, and the connection snapped into place before there were even words for it.

After that I waited. I thought she would tell me, that I would find her crying one afternoon, or that she would take me aside and tell me she needed my help. I couldn't guess what day she told him or what he might have said. I watched her for some sign of doubt or pain, but all I saw was a quiet moodiness, and once or twice, a forced cheerfulness that suddenly turned too giddy, tinged with hysteria.

As I waited and there was no dramatic change, I began to wonder what would happen. There was no visible sign of her pregnancy. I wondered who he was. The man Rupert had seen her with? What if she ran off with him and nobody but me knew why? I imagined the police questioning me, asking if I knew any reason why she might have disappeared. David would return and press me about what I knew. The children would cry and ask me where their mother was and why she had left. I told myself that Charlotte would never leave her family, but every time I convinced myself, I read something in the newspaper about an ordinary citizen committing some unbelievable crime or unnatural act.

My routine had a different feel when I thought about what loomed below the surface. In the mornings I got up early and brought in the milk left at the kitchen door. I liked the thick glass bottles, the layer of cream on top. I thought how antiseptic Safeway's fluorescence seemed by comparison. I fixed toast with Marmite or Golden Syrup for Cary, then walked her along the narrow tarmac road, past the stone church and faded whitewashed cottages, to the grade school with its construction paper cutouts pasted in the windows.

One morning I returned to find Charlotte sitting in the kitchen, still in her bathrobe. She turned on the kettle, then turned it off without fixing anything. Her wrists looked fragile, her hair limp and darker, drained of its brightness. I wanted to make some gesture of sympathy. By now I understood that she didn't want me to know because it would somehow enlarge everything, make it worse. But I couldn't help it any longer.

"Charlotte, is there anything I can do?" I asked.

I knew I was treading over the line of what was supposed to be unspoken.

"No." She looked away from me. She sounded like she was going to cry.

"I wish I could help."

"Help! How could you help?" She turned to me and her voice was furious. It echoed off the kitchen walls, into the hallways and rose up through the empty house. "What could you possibly do to help! I'm stuck with a husband who goes anywhere he wants, who leaves me in this barn of a house with no one but *children* for company."

Charlotte put her head in her hands and started to cry. I moved to touch her hair but she pushed me away. I understood then that I was not a friend; her interest had all been flattery and need. When she looked up again, her face was flat and ugly with tears.

"You can't understand it. You can leave here. You have everything in front of you." She got up quickly, pulled her wrapper around her, and ran out of the room.

I stayed in the kitchen for a few minutes, not knowing what to do. I wanted to cry myself, but I also felt a dark, clear space inside me that had not been there before. I went upstairs to practice, but

I was too unnerved to concentrate. I sat by the window, holding my violin, and stared at the slate and thatched roofs of the village. Charlotte left before lunch without saying good-bye. I tried to practice again in the afternoon. Cary was with a friend, and Rupert was visiting the ponies with Helen. A little after three, I heard the crunch of gravel in the driveway and saw Charlotte's car pull in. From my window I saw a tall, slender man get out of the driver's side. He went around and helped Charlotte get out.

I met them in the entrance hall as he opened the front door. They stood close together, without touching. She must have told him about me because he quickly moved toward me, introduced himself.

"Mrs. Beresford fainted at work. I wanted to make sure she got home all right." He looked at me steadily, not knowing how much I'd already guessed. I held his eyes for a long moment; they were brown with light glints in them, a shade lighter than hers.

"Poor Charlotte." I touched her on the arm, smiled to reassure her, then turned back to him. "Why don't you take her upstairs?"

"I do need to find a way to get back." He looked around the entrance hall, as if for a route of escape.

"I'll find a cab to take you where you need to go—it might take a little time, some of the drivers don't like to come all the way out here," I said.

Charlotte's eyes filled as I delivered this matter-of-fact lie. There was a sodden old cabbie who spent most of his day at the pub, waiting for the odd fare, and I knew it.

I went to the kitchen and put on the kettle. I called for a cab and told them to come in a half hour. He came downstairs twenty minutes later and said he would wait for the cab at the end of the lane. He would have been handsome if he had not looked so upset. I wanted to keep him there for a moment, to hear him talk. I wanted to know what they had together. He was young, perhaps in his early thirties. There were circles under his eyes. He was anxious to get out of the house.

"Well, thank you for getting her back to us," I said.

"Oh, no trouble at all." He smiled nervously and let himself out the kitchen door.

I went upstairs to check on Charlotte. She was already asleep.

In her fist she clenched a plastic orange vial, a prescription for a sedative, like a sleeping child holds a rattle. She curled up the same way Cary did.

When the children arrived, noisy and hungry, I told them their mother had fainted at work. She was sleeping and I was making them dinner myself. The menu was pancakes.

"Pancakes for dinner?" Cary was thrilled.

"Why are we having pancakes for dinner?" Rupert was already suspicious of odd good fortune.

"I don't know, I feel like it."

And I did. It was over. It had not been my waiting, and yet I had waited, and wondered, without the benefit of sure knowledge.

Charlotte slept through the night. When she woke late the next morning, I made her tea and toast with Golden Syrup like I did for Cary. When we were alone, she made no pretense about her condition, and she allowed herself to be cared for, a tacit apology for her outburst the day before.

Lying in bed that night, I thought how David would never know about her affair, or about the baby that had not been born. I thought about Charlotte, and how strange it was to be married to someone who did not know such a large thing about you. And then I felt afraid, because I knew that life was full of these things that matter so enormously and make us what we are—but remain unsaid because to voice them does not make them go away, and instead shakes everything around us apart.

Momentum

Mostly, Jorie tries not to think about it, but recently, Karla's voice has taken up one side of the debate that has echoed back and forth in Jorie's head for years. They have come to know this topic so well that their discussions have become tinged with the familiarity of an old domestic argument. Jorie told her about it all a long time ago, when they were first dating. Now, it has become a kind of open secret between them, the whole reason Jorie is the person who she is.

At thirteen she was called Marjorie. She can't remember what it felt like to be that age; it was as if an unfamiliar child inhabited her body. She remembers turning sixteen, seventeen, she remembers the outlines of her life: her teachers, the seasonal rotation of sports, but she always feels surprised when her friends talk about their early adolescence because Jorie can't remember what she felt like then or what she'd actually thought about the world.

She remembers everything about Ronnie though—Veronica Mary Harten. Ronnie never let anyone call her that. The Hartens moved in, two houses down the street, when Marjorie was in sixth grade, and from the beginning Marjorie was in awe of her: long, tangly black hair, deep blue eyes; Ronnie was wiry and strong, with the skinny bruised legs of a tomboy. There were two older Harten boys, about the same age as Marjorie's brother, but early on, it was Ronnie who achieved a kind of fame at Pleasantville Middle School. Their homeroom teacher, Mr. Lobosco, was a jovial man who habitually addressed his students by their given names. He had been with the Pleasantville school system for more than thirty years. On her first day she called out: "My name is Ronnie," from the back of the room, but Mr. Lobosco would not be dictated to. Finally, one morning, when she refused to answer during roll call, he walked up to her desk and put his hand on her shoulder. Ronnie slipped out from beneath his heavy palm and bit his hand so hard he shrieked. Marjorie remembers seeing the sharp tendons at the back of Ronnie's skinny knees, the flick of her plaid skirt, as she ran out the door. She was suspended from school for a week, but Mr. Lobosco called her Ronnie when she returned.

Ronnie had what she called Passions and Moods. She would say: "I have a Passion for strawberry ice cream," or "I'm in a Black Mood," and Marjorie knew she wasn't supposed to laugh. To Marjorie it seemed that Ronnie's slender body contained more energy than other peoples'; her pale skin was suffused with a fierce light. But there were also times when Ronnie's energy was dimmed, turned inward. She wouldn't go out, or ride bikes, or play. Marjorie tried to entice her with her favorite things: going over to the aqueduct to watch the minibikers, riding their bicycles to Pace Farm to see the goats and ponies, but on some days Ronnie was listless and silent and could not be persuaded to go out. Instead they talked and played records. Ronnie would sneak into her older brothers' room to borrow albums. Inside a few double covers she showed Marjorie the thin film of brownish dust that she said came from cleaning pot. When Marjorie asked how they did it, Ronnie said she wasn't sure; it was something to do with the seeds. Together they looked at the mysterious album covers and contemplated their strangeness.

What did they talk about? Jorie can't remember. They didn't talk about boys. There were none who intrigued them. So much of what she remembers about that time is visual: their street at winter dusk, the large bare oak trees rising from the wide strip of grass between the road and the sidewalk, bicycles left propped against front gates—abandoned for a squabble or a meal. She remembers playing sports: field hockey practice on the first brisk autumn day when the air outside was cold against her face and the heat from her own body rose up inside a heavy cotton sweatshirt. She remembers gymnastics, learning to do flips on the uneven parallel bars—slowly at first, the teacher spotting her, the cinder block walls of the gym and the polished wooden floor turning upside down, and then faster, the strange sensation of aiming for what she sensed but could not see, knowing she would catch the lower bar, but not exactly knowing how. The bruises on her hips the next day. This is what Jorie remembers.

What did she and Ronnie think about? They both liked pistachio ice cream and disliked Girl Scouts, but Jorie can hardly remember what her ideas were then, as if the thoughts that framed her distinctions were vague and unformed.

There is one day Jorie does remember: a black mood day. Ronnie wouldn't go out, so they stayed in her room and listened to a Uriah Heep album she'd taken from her brothers. Ronnie sat on the floor, her legs stretched out in a V, like a cheerleader warming up.

"I've never told anyone this," she said. This statement always prefaced one of Ronnie's secret plans, which ranged from buying a minibike to going to live with David Bowie and painting all his album covers, which they both agreed were very weird. Ronnie leaned forward over the carpet, her hands stretched out in front of her, fingers splayed so the tendons beneath the skin showed. "I've never told anyone this," she repeated. "But sometimes I think about killing myself." She stared up at Jorie. Her freckles stood out against her white skin.

Jorie can't remember what she said in response. She has played this conversation over in her mind a thousand times, but her response is a blank, a silent gap, like the space between songs on a record. She must have asked some vague question. She hopes that her face registered surprise or disbelief. She can see the image of Ronnie so vividly—the grubby powder-blue sweatshirt she always wore, long, knobby-kneed legs, bruised shins, a small, dark cut just below one knee.

"I mean, I think about how I'd do it." Ronnie's voice was muted, almost flat. She straightened her back and tried to stretch further down. Her uncombed hair spread across her slender back, slipped down toward the floor.

Jorie sat down on Ronnie's bed. The coverlet, lime green with a profusion of pink and yellow flowers, was a pattern she now associates with the sixties when she calls it to mind, but when she tries to picture her response she imagines her open lips, a silent O, superimposed on disordered flowers. She knew that Ronnie said a lot of odd things. She remembers believing in the ferocity of Ronnie's feelings without necessarily taking her ideas very seriously.

The following weekend the Gallaghers went to Syracuse to visit Marjorie's grandmother. By the time they came home, Ronnie had found a way to carry out her plan.

When her parents sat her down in the dining room, herded the other children out, and explained what had happened, Jorie remembers noticing what seemed like the wrong details. They had just gotten new drapes in the dining room. Her mother had been wanting them for a long time. When her parents told her about Ronnie, she thought: "But we just got the new drapes." She fixed her eyes on the heavy ivory-colored fabric. Her mother's voice was low and careful, trying to explain without being too explicit and Jorie felt, for the first time, the tide of panic that would overtake her in the following years. Her heart pounded, sending a hot flush through her neck and face: *guilty, guilty, guilty*. She should have told someone what Ronnie had said. The words rose up in her mouth, hot and tearful, but then she thought *they'll blame me*. She swallowed the words and began to cry.

Marjorie went over and over it in her mind. What did she say to Ronnie? She knows that she didn't try to dissuade her, but it hadn't seemed like something Ronnie would actually do. Ronnie's words had seemed like a secret, a passing dangerous thought, like an impossible dare—not the kind of thing to bother an adult about. Marjorie knew her parents had their own world of concerns that were separate from her own, often imaginary fears, and it seemed that the boundary between these two worlds was delicate, not to be pressed against too hard. And who would she have told? Her mother ran their household with a kind of bemused weariness; she was usually preoccupied with the logistics of feeding and carpooling four children. It never occurred to Jorie to tell Ronnie's mother. Mrs. Harten was a delicate, coiffed version of Ronnie. They had the same pale skin and dark hair, but Mrs. Harten seemed like a pallid model, a trial run for her fierce and serious daughter. Besides, telling Ronnie's mother would have been an impossible betrayal. Jorie might have told one of her own sisters, but Maggie was so much older, older than Kevin, and she was preoccupied with boys and college. Jorie's younger sister, Jennifer, was only a child.

Sometimes I think about how I'd do it. Jorie can't remember Ronnie saying anything more. Apparently she'd chosen the most accessible means: her mother's sleeping pills and her father's bourbon. At the time, Marjorie wasn't aware of the decadent implications. It all seemed terrible and mysterious and practical, in the way Ronnie could be.

In the years following Ronnie, there was a small epidemic of suicides in Westchester. A high school girl lay down on the railroad tracks between Pleasantville and Chappaqua, and the 5:38 out of Grand Central went right over her. Chappaqua was a rich town and the girl's death got all kinds of attention. Suddenly there were lectures at school, articles in magazines about the warning signs of teen suicide. Skinny, vibrant Ronnie was forgotten.

The only thing Jorie has forgotten is exactly what she said—or failed to say—to Ronnie on that day. She has developed a remembering trick that she thinks of like vaulting in gymnastics. She tries to call up a series of memories, flashing through them quickly as if she's running toward the horse, running the images fast enough to gain a momentum that will carry her over the place of blank memory and lead her to a precise recollection of that day. She remembers the overarching, deepening green of their street in summer dusk, the gray flagstone path leading to the Hartens' front door, their cool, shadowed downstairs, the record player in Ronnie's room, its gray-and-white speckled case like a faded composition notebook, Ronnie's flowered coverlet, a poster of Bobby Sherman wearing what looked like a dog collar, although Ronnie professed to hate boys. Jorie runs these images through her mind with increasing speed so that when she arrives at that final image of Ronnie, her legs splayed out, leaning forward over the carpet, she will remember exactly what she'd said to Ronnie on that day.

She never told anyone in her family. She never told a priest because the Hartens belonged to their church. Jorie was afraid that, even in the confessional, the priest would know who she was; he would make her tell that Ronnie had hinted at what she would do. Then everyone would know; everyone would hate her.

I have sinned in my thoughts and in my words, in what I have done and in what I have failed to do. Before Ronnie died, Jorie had repeated the words of the Creed without really hearing them, but afterward, every Sunday, they reminded her that God knew. Confession was for forgiveness, and she'd been taught that God would forgive her, but what about everyone else? She didn't think so. And so she doubled her sin by not confessing it, and every holiday, when she went to confession, she knew she would not tell, and she manufactured a few transgressions, or confessed being mean to Jennifer or avoiding some household chore, and the secret grew inside her until it seemed to displace her former self—and no one seemed to notice. This was the most astounding part, that no one guessed she carried a different, burdened self inside her.

Karla is the only person who's ever pressed her to tell someone who knew Ronnie. As an adult Jorie told a few other friends, and they've always assured her that it wasn't her fault; she was young, how could she have known? But now that she and Karla live together, the endless debate of blame and absolution that Jorie carries on within herself has been exposed.

"This may be selfish on my part," Karla says, "but I hate watching you like this. You could try to give yourself a break. Who knows? You might even try to be happy."

"And you think saying something to the Hartens will do that for me?"

"Yes."

"But what if I go there, and tell them, and they're awful?"

Karla sighs, "I don't know. But what's the worst they can do? Cry, get angry, make you feel guilty? I honestly don't know if anyone could make you feel worse than you already do. I'm not saying it will be like the Waltons and everyone will hug each other, but you've never said a word to anyone who knew her. And that's what's eating at you."

"Well, it's easy to figure out someone else's life," Jorie says.

"Of course it is," Karla tells her.

Karla is whole; she doesn't keep secrets. This is what Jorie loves about her. Karla manages the Food Store at Integral Yoga, down in the West Village. She is the woman who Jorie once imagined she could become. For years, Jorie imagined that one day she would be unburdened; she would move through her life with an ease tempered by a knowing gravity. When she was younger, practicing on the uneven parallels, she remembers allowing the weight of her own spinning body to carry her forward through the air, sending her to the next bar. But as she grew older and her guilty preoccupations over almost every act became worse instead of better, nothing seemed to carry her forward, and it seemed the most she could hope for was a lover who possessed the qualities that she herself did not.

Jorie had spent her twenties waiting for the right time to come out to her family. Instinctively, she waited for her siblings to do something more upsetting, so that when she told her parents, it wouldn't seem so earth-shattering. And of course, things did happen. Maggie's husband discovered cocaine, and after only two years of marriage, Maggie took their baby, Christopher, and left. Her brother Kevin, who'd gone into her father's plumbing business, had an affair with a married woman, a customer. When the husband found out, he went down to the office and made a terrible scene. It was a real family scandal—especially because Kevin wasn't apologetic. He said he was in love.

When Jorie finally came out to her parents, she couldn't tell them what seemed like the real secret. As she was saying what she'd rehearsed so often, her voice sounded like an unfamiliar tape recording, and somehow she hoped that her parents would bring up Ronnie, that they would ask her if Ronnie had ever hinted at what she would do. Of course they didn't. It was only within Jorie that the secrets were intertwined. She had expected that her coming out would relieve her floating guilt, but telling her parents seemed almost anticlimactic. They were visibly upset, but kind. They hadn't wanted to suspect what her sisters and Kevin had known for years. She could see, in her mother's eyes, questions that her mother couldn't entirely frame yet.

Afterward, she had hoped her anxiety would ease, that one day she would wake up and feel mysteriously forgiven, but she is thirty-four now, and as she gets older, her anxiousness is getting worse instead of better. At the office, if she doesn't find a document in its expected place, she feels a tightness in her throat, a guilty panic building up inside her. She can't stop looking until she finds what she needs. She knows it's irrational; she's never lost anything of importance; but paperwork left undone, even neatly stacked in an in-basket, presses on her invisibly. She jokes about freelancing as an organizational consultant, putting her obsessiveness to profitable use. But every time she feels that rising panic, and then finds whatever she's looking for, she feels a kind of self-disgust, because she knows her guilt is unreasonable, because she has tried, for years, to talk her way, or think her way, into feeling better. She has to change. She somehow needs to *be* different. And it's the little things that trip her up.

Jorie stands in front of her bedroom mirror holding a new dress in front of her. It was a frivolous purchase, a party dress; it cost too much money. She'll never wear it to work.

"I shouldn't have bought this. I'm going to return it," Jorie says out loud.

Karla walks into the room while Jorie examines the dress in the mirror. "You're so damn guilty about everything," Karla says. "You feel guilty about what you spend, what you don't, what you eat, what you don't. I don't know how you live inside your own skin. Sometimes—" she pauses and then softens her voice. "So much of your life is about keeping things in order. Keeping everything intact. I mean, look, you became an accountant. You want everything to come out right, neat and tidy, pay what you owe, so nothing bad will happen. Cover every base because this one thing got away from you—and Jesus, you were just a kid."

Jorie feels her face crumple and she starts to cry. She can't help it. She is tired of thinking about it, tired of the endless debates she carries on within herself.

"She didn't tell you she was going to do it. She told you she thought about it. At thirteen you're supposed to be a shrink or something?"

Marjorie takes a deep breath. Was that what Ronnie said? By now she can hardly remember.

Jorie gets up and goes to the window. Even in the city, the sky has the gray density of coming snow. At Thanksgiving, her parents announced they were putting the house on the market. This would probably be the last family Christmas in the house. The Hartens still live down the street. She imagines spending her whole life running through her catalog of images, trying to remember what she said, trying to release herself from that day. She feels a pressure behind her eyes. She has to tell them.

Jorie stands in the door of their apartment with her Christmas gifts and an overnight bag. Karla has a nineteen-year-old son who's coming for Christmas, and Jorie wishes she was staying with them, that she was not about to make this particular trip home.

"I'm terrified," Jorie says.

"I know."

Jorie sees the hesitation in Karla's eyes. Now that she is actually going to go through with it, she sees that Karla is scared. But having decided, the idea of backing out seems worse.

"I'll let you know what happens," Jorie says.

Karla nods, then pulls her close and kisses her on the forehead like a child.

Pleasantville. The name had never seemed ironic until Jorie grew up and moved away. She sets her shopping bag of presents on the seat next to her and settles in by the window. The train is only half full in the middle of the day. She looks out through the scratched, dirty windows into the dark tunnels of New York. How does the city support all its skyscrapers? What does Manhattan rest on, with so much of it burrowed out underneath?

The train moves slowly through the tunneled darkness, coming up into the desolate streets around 125th Street. She tries to imagine going to the Hartens' house. What will she say? Out of habit she closes her eyes and tries to think of details that will lead her back to that day. Ronnie wanted a minibike. Her brothers each had one, and after school, and on weekends, they rode along the aqueduct road or the powerline trails. Ronnie never said much about her brothers, but she had begged her father for a minibike, one fast enough, she said, to outrun them. When her father gave her a new bicycle that Christmas, with a long banana seat, all the rage then, and tassels hanging from its handlebars, Ronnie was furious. "It's a girl's bike," she said angrily, her face white and pinched. She wouldn't even try it out. "That's not the point," she kept saying. Marjorie didn't understand Ronnie's vehemence, but then, Ronnie could be that way.

At Valhalla the train leans to the left when they stop; it has always tilted here; she wonders why. From the train window she can see the Sinclair station and a few shops; the base of the dam is hidden behind the trees. As a child, the vast granite expanse of the Valhalla Dam was the largest thing she'd ever seen. There was a traffic circle below it, and she remembers riding in the car on the way to her grandmother's, running her fingertips along the textured vinyl seat, praying the dam would stay up as they passed below it. The train straightens up as it leaves Valhalla. Spindly gray forest, Bronx River Parkway, Gate of Heaven Cemetery; her grandparents are buried there. The stonecutter's store is visible from the train.

Jennifer is waiting for her at the Pleasantville train station. She is twenty-seven now, living in D.C., full of political gossip that Jorie doesn't completely understand. At home, everyone seems much the same, and yet, they're all getting older. Kevin's dark curly hair shows more than a little gray. He and her father are reserved around each other. Maggie has a new job. The baby is the center of attention.

Jorie puts her bags upstairs in the room she once shared with Jennifer. Whenever she comes back, she is struck by how small the room seems. Sloping ceilings, fluffy bedspreads, dust ruffles; it's hard to imagine she lived in this room. She associates it with the suffocating secrecy of adolescence, the nights when she wanted to confess to Jennifer in the dark.

Every year the Hartens have a Boxing Day party, a kind of neighborhood open house. She can't go to the party knowing what she has to tell them. She feels a wave of anxiety wash through her and she sits on the edge of her bed. She feels almost nauseous; there's a pressure building up inside her head, a pressing behind her eyes. She leans forward and puts her head between her legs. When she can sit up without feeling dizzy, she takes her coat and slips out of the house.

She walks up the Hartens' flagstone path. Everything looks the same. Standing at the front door, she hopes, for an instant, they won't be home. Maybe they've moved away. At this idea she feels a vague panic; she might never get the chance to tell. Her eyes feel hot. She presses the doorbell and Mrs. Harten answers the door.

"Marjorie, what a surprise! How are you? Come in."

Jorie follows her into the house, which is darkened, quiet.

"Come back to the kitchen. I've got something on the stove." She leans her slender body up into the stairway and calls out. "Bill, Marjorie Gallagher is here."

There is silence, then Jorie hears the rustling of a newspaper, footsteps on the floor above.

Mr. Harten appears on the stairs. He seems older, a little heavier, his square face starting to fall. He had been a handsome man. It was something she'd never realized.

"You're a little early for the party, Margie," he says, smiling at her.

"Come on back here, I've got to keep an eye on the stove," Mrs. Harten says.

Jorie follows her toward the kitchen.

"Can I get you something to drink? A little sherry, a glass of wine?" Mr. Harten pauses by the sideboard in the dining room. Jorie remembers these bottles with the little silver name plates on chains around their necks: gin, vodka, bourbon. She remembers Ronnie saying that her brothers stole drinks when their parents weren't home.

"Sherry, please."

He hands her a small, bell-shaped glass and they walk into the kitchen. Mrs. Harten is standing at the stove, frying meatballs in a pan. Jorie wants to summon them into the dining room or living room, somehow make this announcement with a sense of gravity, but she's afraid she will panic if she has to wait any longer.

"I have to tell you something," she blurts out.

Mr. Harten hears the change in her voice and looks up; Mrs. Harten turns away from the stove to look at her.

"I never told you this because Ronnie told me it was a secret," Jorie says. She feels her face get hot; something in her vision is distorted, as if the corners of the kitchen walls are slightly curved, bending in toward the center. "Once, one afternoon, Ronnie told me that . . . she told me that she thought about how she'd kill herself. I mean, she didn't tell me what she was thinking, or how she was going to do it. She said it was a secret, an idea."

Mrs. Harten rests the spatula on the stovetop.

"So she told you it was a secret?" Her tone is not questioning, but flat, a statement of fact.

Jorie feels her hands start to shake. She nods.

Mr. Harten looks at her. "Jesus, Margie." He rubs his face with his palm. "I guess we should have talked to you, but . . ." his voice is quiet. "Listen, it wasn't a secret. At all. She said it to us too."

Jorie feels a shock, her whole body cold, like a dive into freezing water.

"You know that time she bit the math teacher?" Mr. Harten's voice is low, explaining, as if this is the beginning of a hesitantly told, but familiar story. "We were supposed to put her on some medication, but—"

"That was not it!" Mrs. Harten's voice is mean, white with barely suppressed anger. "Medicine never had anything to do with it."

Mr. Harten assumes an expression Jorie has never seen; his jowls harden, his whole face thickens. Almost instantly, he's become a red so deep that Jorie is afraid for him. He looks as if he's choking.

"It wasn't medicine, her brothers—" Mrs. Harten says.

"You don't know that!" The pans suspended on a rack above him make a dull tingling in the wake of his shout. Jorie feels rocked by the force of their anger in a room that appears utterly still. They stand there awkwardly, listening to the faint metallic echo. He takes an openmouthed breath, trying to compose himself.

"The school psychiatrist wanted to put her on drugs, some medication. We talked about it and talked about it." He looks at his wife, who has turned off the stove and stands with her back to them, her hands gripping either side of the stove top. "We decided not to medicate her," he continued. "It was me, mostly—. Valerie wasn't sure. I was against it. You know how Ronnie was. I thought it was just high spirits, hormones or something. The idea of drugs, medication, seemed extreme. I didn't know. I just didn't know."

Jorie stares. She can't quite absorb what he's saying. Ronnie's brothers. She hardly ever talked about them. She said she hated boys. Jorie tries, for a moment, to make it all cohere, but standing between them—Mrs. Harten bracing herself over the stove top, Mr. Harten standing on the other side of the room, his arms crossed in front of him—Jorie understands she will never really know what Ronnie's brothers did, or didn't, do. But it wasn't a secret. She was not the only one who knew. She tries to overlay this knowledge on her past, over everything that's happened since her thirteenth year, but it's too much to absorb. She thinks of a day at work when someone ran "spell check" over a document written in Swedish and the computer just went nuts. She is ashamed to feel a sense of vast relief, a relief so large it could be mistaken for emptiness. She knows she should say something, but she can't imagine what. They're quiet for a moment and Jorie can only come back to what has obsessed her for years.

"She told you too?" Jorie asks again.

"Yes," he answers.

Jorie walks down the front steps and hesitates, then picks her way down the flagstone path. When she reaches the front gate, she turns to look down her street, past her house, out toward the main road. She feels weighted but unmoored, as if something deep inside her has been cast off, but her body still feels the weight of what she carried. She is overwhelmed by a terrible sense of waste; she wants to cry for her foolishness, for the hours and hours and hours she spent thinking about that day. She thinks of all the ways she tried to remember, the litany of images and sensations recalled over and over, like an incantation or charm that would open memory's door: this view of the neighborhood, the bare trees at dusk, the smell of weather turning cold, and flying between the uneven parallel bars, aiming for what she sensed, but could not see, the inexplicable momentum that carried her when finally she let go.

Theodolite

There are some things you know walking into them, and even from the beginning, part of me knew that Sarah's mysterious privacies were beyond me, but I've lived most of my life in and around Ventura, and I guess the hazy light and soft air make me optimistic. If you've never been to southern California, the first thing you probably think of is the beach, but the weather and topography are more complex than blue skies and sand. Contrary to what the song says, it does rain in California, and the mountains are as much a presence as the ocean. I work as a surveyor for Caltrans, which builds and maintains the roads, and my work allows me the illusion that the world—or at least its surface—is measurable and knowable. We also plan for disasters, and given the likelihood of earthquakes and fires, I know that certain things can be avoided through measuring and planning, through understanding the lay of the land. But the collisions of certain lives are almost inescapable, and Sarah happening to me was as inevitable as the rain.

It was a Friday night, payday, and a few of us on the crew decided to get some dinner at a place in Santa Monica. From the bar it seemed your average kind of restaurant, dark and cool, but the hostess led us into the dining room where a girl was singing from a small, elevated platform set against the back wall. On the far side of the makeshift stage was a baby grand piano; she was accompanied by a man I couldn't see. The girl had straight, shiny brown hair that sort of fell into her face, and when she finished her song, a slow, melancholy melody that made me think of scratchy records and fancy martini glasses, she nodded as people clapped and her bright hair swayed past her chin and covered her face. She didn't make any cute comments between songs. Leaning over the microphone, she opened her lips and dipped toward the mike. I felt a shimmering gap in that expectancy, a silence that made the clink of silverware, my friends' voices, and everything around me disappear. She sang in a low, breathy kind of voice, as if the words were dark and indelibly private, as if she were singing softly to herself, wanting only to be overheard, rather than perform. She called the song that followed "White Girl's Blues," and as she sang it, not hamming it up and acting all soulful, but quiet and understated, it seemed that she was reaching into some unlit part of herself. The melody settled around her like smoke.

In truth, I couldn't say whether she was really good or not. I watched the crowd to gauge my reaction. They paid attention, or respectfully ate their dinners; there seemed to be a general acknowledgement that she was worth listening to. She closed her eyes when she sang, and I saw the curve of her cheek below her eyelashes, how small and delicate she was. She wore a ring on her thumb.

"Huge tits," Doug said. "Beatnik type."

"Christ Dougie, you don't even know what a beatnik is."

"You're besotted. I can tell. Gonna get your end wet?"

"Shut up. Have a beer," I said.

When the song ended and everybody clapped, she looked up

and brushed her hair from her face. She smiled a closemouthed smile, as if something hurt her, a stone in her shoe. We had just caught the end of her set, and when she left the stage I wanted to follow her, but the waitress came and set my steak in front of me. I figured I'd find her after the next break.

But she didn't come back. A bleached blonde with a leathery tan and fishnet stockings got up and sang show tunes. I got up from the table and went to look for the girl in the bar, through the restaurant, but she wasn't there. I even asked the bartender.

"That girl that was singing before. Do you know what happened to her?"

"Never seen her before."

"Will she be back?"

"Can't say. We just started doing this."

When I got back to the table, Dougie slapped me on the shoulder.

"Let's get out of here and drink some beer," he said.

"Sure." I answered, but the evening had gone flat.

I tried to call the restaurant to find out when she'd be back, but the person who booked the singers was never around. After a week had gone by, I decided to go back. That afternoon, Doug and I were paired up again.

"Hey, a friend of mine is having a party up in Goleta. You should come up," he said.

"Maybe another time. My mom is cooking. I'm going home for dinner."

"Suit yourself."

No one who'd eaten at my mother's would ever kid me about going home for a meal. My parents had split up years ago and, although they both still lived in southern California, there had been no doubt in my mind about who I'd choose to live with. We didn't have much money when I was little, but my mother was determined to make us happy and comfortable; my brother and sister and I had grown up on pot roasts and gravy, chicken pot pie, enchiladas, and homemade macaroni and cheese. My mother was a cake decorator by trade, and she baked at home too—angel food cake, holiday cookies, lemon meringue pie made from lemons grown in the backyard.

But I wasn't going to my mother's. I cleaned up after work and headed back to the restaurant. I opened the door and was pushed back by two carpenters carrying a large piece of paneling out the door. I went in and saw the place was being taken apart. A tired-looking woman in a navy blazer was standing behind the bar with a clipboard in her hand.

"Renovating?"

"Selling the place," she sighed. "They're making it into a sushi palace."

"I was looking for a young woman who sang here once."

"Can't help you. The singers were a last-ditch attempt to bring in business. The woman who booked them took off for some job in San Diego."

I thanked her and left. I wondered where the party in Goleta was, but I didn't have the heart for it. The idea of my empty apartment seemed depressing, so I drove. I headed up the Pacific Coast Highway, which wasn't too crowded early on a Friday evening. The mountains were familiar, dark and sheltering; the ocean breeze was comforting. I went to college in Seattle, and I loved the caffeinated expectancy, the different neighborhoods and outdoor markets, the mountains so close to the city, the variations of cloudy gray. When I talked about home, I joked about how southern California was one big patio, how everything seemed to revolve around shopping—as if there were nothing better to do than move from mall to outlet mall, a waste of beautiful weather. But at Christmastime I'd go back to Ventura, or drive down to Point Mugu and up into the canyons above Malibu, remembering a California that had a cyclic, elemental feel: the Santa Ana winds blowing hot in the fall, the avocados ripening in December, the smooth bark of orange trees weighted with fruit, the bottlebrush trees blooming in March, the pyracantha I was allergic to.

I stayed in Seattle for a few years after college, but I moved back here to work for Caltrans. Over the next six years, I measured and surveyed large sections of these roads and I felt proprietary about them. My father worked for Caltrans too, and as much as I hated to admit it, since our relationship was practically nonexistent, I felt an invisible connection with him as I traveled and worked on the same network that he did, a way of connecting without having to keep in touch.

One Saturday morning I was in old-town Ventura, running a few errands with a cup of coffee in hand, when the girl from the restaurant stepped out of a used-clothing store. If I hadn't heard her sing, I might have noticed her only as a somewhat pretty, brown-haired girl. She looked up and down the sidewalk, her expression hesitant. In the late-morning light she looked, for a moment, less mysterious. Without any makeup, her skin was pale. She was small, an unspoken apology in her stance; she didn't stand up quite straight. I wanted to press my palm between her shoulder blades, touch her shoulders, press them back. Her hair was put up, but it escaped from its clip and fell softly around her face. She seemed unsure, birdlike, poised on the sidewalk in Levis and a white T-shirt.

"Hello." I stepped forward and extended my hand.

She looked at me almost fearfully for a moment.

"I heard you sing in a restaurant down in Santa Monica a few weeks ago. I really liked your voice." I sounded stupid, *voice* a silly word to describe what had attracted me.

"You heard me sing?" She looked at me quizzically.

"Yes, I really liked it."

Her hand was warm and dry; she withdrew it.

"Well, that's nice of you to say, but the place closed after I sang there just once, so I guess I didn't exactly bring in business." She laughed a little at her self-deprecation and I saw the reason for her closemouthed smile: her teeth were crooked, not terribly so, but in this land of nose jobs and braces, she was noticeably snaggletoothed. She caught me noticing and glanced away.

"The food wasn't too good," I said.

She turned back to me and stared me down, amused.

"Listen, would you like to get a cup of coffee or something?" I asked.

She glanced at the Styrofoam container in my hand. "Looks like you're already set."

"Yeah, well . . ."

"I have to get home and deal with this stuff." She indicated the plastic bag in her hand, then seemed to reconsider me. "Maybe a cup wouldn't hurt. There's a place right up here."

We walked down the sidewalk with the bag bumping between us. Inside the shop, we settled ourselves on some stools and I bought her a coffee and chose some pastries at random.

"So I guess you're from around here," she said.

"I grew up about ten miles south of here. What about you?"

She jerked her thumb north, as if hitchhiking. "North. Oregon really, but that was a while ago."

"So are you down here trying to be a singer?"

She winced. "*Trying* is about it."

I felt terrible then, worse later, when I realized that more than anything else, being a singer was really what she aspired to. She didn't have any money or connections, so she took whatever singing jobs she could, hoping somehow, and foolishly she knew, to be discovered.

"It's unusual to hear someone singing the kind of music you do."

"It's what I like."

The coffee shop was bright, everything labeled in Italian. We looked out at the people walking by: transients, old hippies, rich people, and college kids. She parried most of my questions in a manner so subtle that I didn't realize, until after I left her, how little I knew, but I could tell by the failing momentum of our conversation that I was making a mistake by asking too many questions.

"Are you singing anywhere now?"

"No, I don't have anything lined up."

"Can I ask for your phone number?"

"Well, you can ask." She stared out the shop window intently. "I don't usually give my number to guys I meet on the street. Why don't you give me your number and I can call you?"

There wasn't much I could say to that, so we patted ourselves down and fumbled around for pens and paper. I finally went up to the register where the cashier handed me a receipt slip and a pen.

I wrote out my name and number carefully, and handed the slip to her. "Maybe we could have dinner some night?" I asked.

"I'll give you a call."

She took the slip of paper from my hand. Her fingers were thin, her fingernails bitten.

"Later on," she said, and hoisted her bag onto her shoulder.

I watched her walk away.

She didn't call. I had never imagined myself as the type to hover by the phone, but whenever I went out, I worried that I'd miss her. I'd had a girlfriend for years, and Patty was wonderful, but from the beginning she had her eye on marriage and kids. She loved my family, especially my mother. Actually, I believed that Patty wanted to be a younger, sexier version of my mother. She borrowed recipes from her, learned to make some of the same dishes, but I couldn't imagine proposing. When she finally gave me an ultimatum, I felt cruel when I didn't even need to consider the terms.

"I'm sorry." I told her. "But I won't be bullied into proposing. What kind of way is that to begin a marriage?"

And she left. As she should have. That had been more than a year ago, and although I found myself missing the sex, mostly I was relieved. There were lots of women I found pleasurable to watch, but there wasn't anyone who seemed worth the trouble of what you'd call a relationship. My older sister would often, with a relative lack of subtlety, bring a single friend to one of the large and casual parties my mother threw to mark our birthdays, Labor Day, Memorial Day, and other occasions, but these women were heavy with the obligation of being friends of my sister's, which involved more baggage than I wanted. A few had been so horny that they weren't especially appealing. The last time my sister brought a friend to a big party, the woman had followed me into the garage where I was getting beer out of a refrigerator my mother kept for extras. I was bending into the fridge when I thought I heard the garage door click shut. I heard the turn of the deadbolt being locked. I straightened up without saying anything. She sidled past one car, came to stand in front of me, then rested her weight on her palms and pushed herself up to sit on the hood of my mother's ancient station wagon. She had long curly hair that was unexpectedly hard to the touch, and her perfume was cloying and strong, but it was hard to argue with the way she wrapped her legs around me and slid her hands under my T-shirt.

I was wondering whether, if we continued, we'd actually dent the hood of the car when one of my little nephews started banging on the door, "Orange soda, orange soda, bring us orange soda!" he yelled.

"Shit." I muttered. And although I was frustrated, later I was grateful, knowing it wouldn't be the smartest thing to poke some horny hairsprayed friend of my sister's in my mother's garage.

Finally, a week later, Sarah called.

"I thought I'd take you up on that dinner offer," she said.

She said she'd meet me in Ventura; she was busy that day and it would be the easiest thing for her. I wondered why I couldn't pick her up at home.

I took her to a place called Neptune's Net, at the base of the Santa Monica Mountains, right near the beach in north Malibu. The food was good, but it wasn't too fancy. I didn't want to scare her off. The sunset was undramatic that night. A few dark kites twisting and dipping over the ocean like bats, the canyons darkening blue.

She seemed to relax in the bustle of the restaurant, which catered to a varied clientele: Ken and Barbie types as well as bikers, suburbanites from Thousand Oaks.

"So why did singing bring you to LA? Why not Chicago? New York?"

"People told me college was important. I wanted to establish residency so I could go to school," she said. "I went to UCSB for a couple of semesters, but it was hard to pay rent, tuition, and all that. I had to take time off to earn money, and after a while, I don't know, it just started to seem endless. It wasn't really what I wanted to do anyway. I wanted to study music and composition theory, but I hated having to pay for all the general requirements before I could get to what I wanted."

"Couldn't your parents help you out?"

"No." She set down her fork and looked out toward the ocean. She stared out over the water for a full minute, then she seemed to relent.

"When I first came down here I was knocked out by . . ." she stopped and giggled. "This will sound silly, but I couldn't get over the palm trees—in parking lots. It seemed so strange. The palm trees and the weather, so many people in nice clothes, this place seemed like paradise."

"Still feel that way?"

"Not so much. I've done a lot of temping, cocktail waitressing. And waitressing you meet so many people who've come here trying to act or sing or write for the movies. You'd be surprised at how few regular types I meet."

"So I'm a regular type?"

"Yes, you are."

"I hope that doesn't mean I'm boring."

"No, not necessarily." She smiled a little half-smile.

We took our time over dinner, and when we were done with our meal she sat back in her chair.

"You can't smoke in a restaurant in this whole damn county." She pushed her hair back from her face, as if squaring off for a fight.

"A singer and you smoke?"

"Less than I used to. It's my one weakness."

I paid the check and debated what to do next. She seemed more relaxed, but I knew better than to ask her back to my place, and since she hadn't even let me pick her up, I doubted she was going to invite me back to hers.

"Still want a cigarette? We can go down to the beach."

"Okay."

We drove up the highway, the night sky pale orange behind the looming mountains, the ocean a darker shimmering I sensed but couldn't see. I pulled off near Point Mugu. She let herself out of the car and immediately leaned against it, cupped her hand against the wind, and lit a cigarette. She started walking toward the ocean ahead of me, then stopped to let me catch up.

"It's freezing out here," she said.

Standing behind her, I put my arms around her and put my face in her hair. Sweetness and smoke. She dropped her cigarette in the sand.

"Bury it now," I said. "No fires here."

She quashed it with her foot.

"Do you always go around telling girls what to do?"

She turned in my arms and reached up to me. I bent to kiss her, and felt something when I touched her that had never quite happened before. I had always thought of kissing as something almost obligatory, something I did on the way to something else, but this was like nothing I'd ever felt, a kind of wordless conversation where I finally didn't have to be careful about what I said or asked.

We stayed there for a while, but I could feel she was freezing and I took her back to the car.

"Are you going to let me drop you at home?"

"Yes." Her voice was quiet.

I didn't want to push it. In truth, I felt a little shaky myself. She directed me to some nice condos in Ventura and I pulled up in front of her door.

I leaned over to kiss her good night. Again there was that connection that made me want to climb over the stick shift and bury myself in her.

She put her hands along my face.

"I should go," she said.

I waited until she got inside her apartment before leaving. Halfway home I realized that I'd forgotten to ask for her number and I groaned to myself out loud.

She didn't call the next day. I couldn't believe it. I kept looking for her in places I knew she couldn't be, as if there were a chance she would step out from behind a hill, or magically appear as she had that morning in Ventura. She'd told me her last name was Jameson, but she wasn't listed in the phone book. At work we were surveying a section of the highway near the beach, and peering through the transit, I spotted a couple of kids messing around on the beach. The transit magnified things almost like binoculars, and I couldn't stand to look at those kids. Why hadn't she called me? What if she was living with someone? What if she was married? The thought made my stomach drop, like hitting a bump in the road.

"Shit, you're foggy today," Doug said at lunch.

"Went out with that girl, that singer from the restaurant."

"No shit. How'd you find her?"

"Ran into her in Ventura."

"Well, she must be something. You can't even see straight. But then, you have all the luck. I thought Patty was pretty damn cute."

"No comparison."

And there wasn't. Patty had been an open book. Sweet, practical, her idea of an exciting evening was going out and buying some fancy underwear at Victoria's Secret, which she then felt self-conscious about wearing. But if Patty was sunny and open, appealing for a kind of healthy transparency, then Sarah's rainy interiority was dark and full and unexpected.

Sarah finally did call a few days later, but she continued to be reticent about where she worked, how she afforded her rent, who her nonexistent parents were. The third time we went out, she came home with me. That night made my years with Patty seem like a pale imitation of what sex was. Part of it was pent-up longing, I suppose, and part of it was wanting to break down the silence that Sarah hid behind. For all her withholding of facts and information, her touch was deliberate and articulate, almost frighteningly exploratory. And late in the night, when she told me she couldn't come anymore, and she did, one final time, she cried in my arms and I ran my hand along her back and her shoulder blades and she fell asleep like that, holding onto me. We hardly moved until morning, when we untangled ourselves and fell back to sleep until late.

The next day was Saturday, and as I made her breakfast, she sat in my one decent kitchen chair, quiet, almost chastened.

"What would you like to do today?" I asked. "Do you want to go somewhere?"

"Okay, but I have to be home around four o'clock."

"What do you have to do?" The question was offhand. I thought I could ask her anything now, but she stiffened a little and looked down into her coffee. I felt the delicate thread between us snap.

"I can't believe this." I set the coffeepot down on the counter. "You can't even tell me what the deal is with you? Are you married? Living with someone? Was last night a kind of common occurrence for you?"

She rested her forehead on the table. "I'm not married for godsakes."

I waited.

"Well—" she picked her head up, snuffling a bit. I handed her a napkin. "I live with this guy named Bernard. He's gay. I'm kind of a cover for him. He's got a really conservative job, and it just helps him if he can bring a date along to certain things. I have to go up to Ojai for drinks this afternoon."

"Oh come on. This is California. 1997. It's fucking fashionable to be gay. He could sue the pants off anyone who discriminated against him."

"It's not that simple. He's in private banking; it's a family-owned company. He loves his job. He's not a . . . confrontational type."

"So I'm supposed to believe—"

"You believe what you want to, but if you're going to be like this, I don't see what the point is." She got up and headed to the bedroom.

I watched her walk away, then I followed her into the bedroom. She stood over the bed with her clothes in her arms, her shoulders shaking. When I put my arms around her, she pulled away.

"Listen to me," she said. "I'm just not one of those people who spills out their life to everyone. I'm not. But I want you to understand this, and I will say this only once—" she stood up taller; her voice was almost menacing. "I do not lie. Do you understand that? I would not lie to you—or to anyone. So don't try to put me into that position or I will leave." She sat down on the bed. "Bernard is a lovely man. He's probably the only person in the world who believes I can be a singer. He came into a place I was singing one night, and then he came back to hear me again. We started to talk between sets, he brought friends and dates to hear me, and it just kind of worked out. They were starting to wonder about him at work, and of course he's going to come out to them at some point, but he's getting established and he just wants a little friction-free time in his life. Can you blame someone for that? Good Christ, is a little bit of *peace* so much to ask?" She shook with anger as her question trembled in the air. "And my car had just broken down for the hundredth time, and I'd maxed out my Visa paying for repairs, and once again I was broke, and Bernard asked if I wanted to move in with him. I have dinner out with him and clients. He said I could just contribute what was workable and it would be fine. So we have an arrangement."

"Oh, God, I had no idea." I crouched at the foot of the bed and put my head on her knees.

Over the next few weeks, as we spent more time together, I began to understand how much I had upset her shelter and perhaps, although she'd never call it that, the appearance of a rise in class. Bernard ate at nice restaurants, golfed with his clients, and although I knew practically nothing about Sarah's family, I didn't think country clubs were part of the picture. She could talk about his golf game with the bored affection of a spouse. Sarah and I quickly became what I suppose you'd call a couple, but there were tacit stipulations. I brought her to meet my mother, but cautioned my mother about asking her anything too personal. Bernard apparently knew about me, because I finally had Sarah's phone number, but I had never been invited inside his apartment.

One evening, when I knocked on her door, there was no answer. I knocked again and waited. I'd spoken to her the day before. I wondered where she could be. I stood at the door, half-angry, half-frightened, and rang the bell. A light breeze moved the branches of a bottlebrush tree; the delicate cylindrical shadows swayed back and forth on the wall.

Sarah finally opened the door. She looked muddled and vague, as if she'd just had bad news.

"Come in," she said.

I stepped forward into an elegantly appointed apartment: leather couches, black metal lamps, very modern. Sarah, chameleonlike, seemed to fit here in an urban sort of way.

"We have to talk." She led me over to one of the cool sofas in the shadowed room. I sat down, preparing to hear she was a Russian spy, the child of an underground fugitive, someone stolen by the gypsies.

"I'm pregnant." Her expression was serious, certainly not happy. In the darkened room I couldn't read her. I reached for her hand.

"Marry me."

"What?"

"Let's get married. I mean it."

"You can't be serious," she said.

I knew I had to step carefully. "I know it's your body and all that, so finally it's up to you, but I love you, I want to be with you."

"You don't have any idea of what you're getting into."

I sat back and looked at a painting on the wall in front of me, an overlay of colored rectangles that looked abstract enough to be famous.

"You're right," I said. "I don't. But I'm willing to try."

She looked at me for a long moment, as if measuring me, trying to decide if I was a good bet.

"Let's think of it this way," and I lowered my voice. "Do you want to get rid of it?"

She looked away and tightened her mouth. I knew she was wishing for a cigarette.

"I had an abortion almost ten years ago," she said. "I was going off to *college*. They tell you it's not so bad, but it is."

I pulled Sarah close. Her life seemed so precarious; I couldn't imagine her any more vulnerable. I wasn't thinking about the baby then. I didn't feel proprietary about something I could barely imagine.

She twisted her fingers in her lap and her hair fell across her face.

"Sarah, look at me. Do you want to get married?"

If she had hedged at that moment, I would have been humiliated, and backed down, but she nodded, mute, and then kissed me.

"Yes," she said. "Let's get married."

I held her and kissed her, knowing I had captured someone exceedingly rare. I wouldn't have to contend with that wall of separation, to carefully tiptoe through the minefield of what was permissible to ask.

"Do you want us to look for a new apartment? Mine isn't bad, but it's not as nice as this."

"I can't imagine doing anything as ambitious as looking for an apartment," she sighed. "I'm tired like you wouldn't believe. I was incredibly nervous before you came, and I still fell asleep."

"What did you think I'd say?"

"Honestly, I couldn't stand to think. I had no idea."

"How do you want to get married?" I ran my finger down her arm.

"I hate the idea of people looking at me. I don't have anyone to invite anyway—except Bernard and a few of his friends. Let's just go to the courthouse or whatever it is that people do."

I didn't know whether to feel hurt or relieved. Whenever Patty had started gushing about a friend's wedding, I'd felt annoyed at the implied plans she had for our own event. I tried to quell my hurt at Sarah's lack of sentiment.

"What about your parents?" I asked.

"Why bother?"

"What's that supposed to mean?"

She looked away and I felt as if I were going into a mine with a candle, watching for the faintest sign that would snuff the light out.

"Sarah, I've tried to respect your privacy, but give me a little bit of a break. I don't care what your family is like, but I need to know why you don't want to talk about them."

She took a deep breath. "I haven't been in touch with my mother for a couple years now. What do you want me to tell you? She lives in a trailer and drinks warm vodka and smokes cigarettes. That's pretty much my mother's existence. Or it was. Last I heard she had a trache—one of those operations for cancer of the throat. I called after the operation and talked to one of the nurses. I don't think my mother can even talk anymore. Or she's got one of those scary sounding machines."

"Sarah, that's terrible."

"She probably smokes out of the hole." Sarah looked me straight in the eye. "That's what I come from."

We just sat still after that, then Sarah stretched out against me and I slid back on Bernard's couch.

"Just stay here with me for a while, okay?" she said.

She settled against me and I shifted my arm as it started to fall asleep. She began to doze in the shadowed room, and I lay there trying to absorb it all. She was right. I had no idea what I was getting into. It was hard to imagine a baby. I thought about an engagement ring. I wanted to buy her one. She would protest, but I guessed she'd secretly be pleased.

"What about your mother?" Sarah mumbled.

"My mother will be tickled."

"She'll think I trapped you."

"No she won't, she likes you."

"Your mother likes everyone."

"That's not true." Although I knew what Sarah meant. My mother would be caught off guard by news of a marriage, but she'd be thrilled about the baby.

"Let's go tell her." I felt a thread of nervousness at my own suggestion.

"What? Now?"

"Yeah, why not?

"Are you sure?"

"Let me call her and tell her we're stopping by. Where's the—"

Sarah pointed to a stand near the kitchen.

My mother lived in Camarillo, a little town south of Ventura. On the phone I said that Sarah and I had some news for her. I felt a thrum in my stomach, like when I was a kid and I had to own up to something I'd done wrong. Sarah was quiet on the ride down.

"My mother is really nuts about babies."

"I'm nervous."

We pulled up in front of my mother's house and I took Sarah's hand and helped her get out of the car.

"Don't get chivalrous on me," she said.

"I feel that way."

"What? Like you're rescuing me?"

"Oh Jesus, Sarah no." But the truth was I did, a little.

"It does take two you know. I didn't get this way by myself." She leaned back, away from me, against the car.

"Look, let's cut the crap. Are you backing out? If you don't want to get married, then tell me now. If the idea of marrying me is such a drag—"

She put her face in her hands. "I'm sorry, I'm sorry," she mumbled. "I'm afraid your mother is going to hate me for nailing her son."

"Stop, she's not like that." I swallowed back my worries and led her to the door.

My mother had just gotten off work and was still in her white clothes and work shoes; when I was little, I'd thought she was a nurse.

"Come on in," she said. "I feel terrible, having you stop by and I've got nothing special to offer you. We're coming up on Easter and I've been so busy at the store. Do you want something to drink—iced tea?"

She poured us all some drinks and then sat down in her recliner. I could tell she wanted to put her feet up, but she sensed whatever we had to say was not news to be taken leaning back. We sat on the couch opposite her. I took Sarah's hand.

"We've got some pretty exciting news. I've asked Sarah to marry me. We're expecting a baby."

"Oh, oh!" My mother flew forward. She put her hands on either side of Sarah's face and kissed her on both cheeks. "A baby, a baby, oh how wonderful!"

I don't think I'd ever been so grateful to my mother as I was at that moment. Sarah's relief was visible and she blushed beneath my mother's show of emotion. I was even more thankful because my mother, without pretending to ignore the circumstances, didn't press on them either.

"Oh, this is so exciting," she said. "Have you talked about what kind of wedding you'd like to have?"

"I think I hurt Paul's feelings by saying that I wanted to get married at the courthouse." Sarah's voice was quiet, but kind. I felt a little shock at her forthrightness. "To tell you the truth, I don't really have any family to speak of, and the idea of anything bigger just makes all that seem more . . ."

"Of course, of course," my mother said. "Well, what about this? Maybe we could have a little party here afterward? It could be casual or fancy. I don't want to intrude on what you want."

"A party afterward would be great," Sarah said.

We discussed a weekend for the reception. Sarah and my mother discussed food, decorations. My mother kept saying: "Just tell me what you want, and leave it to me." Hearing them murmuring together made me feel as if the answer to a large and worrisome math problem had finally made itself apparent, and the solution had appeared, as if inevitable, before my eyes.

I did have moments of doubt. Mostly at work when I was out in the sun, doing something specific and calculable, when so much about Sarah seemed immeasurable and uncharted. Everything about my job reassured me that even the most turning road could be plotted, its coordinates set down. I'd had an engineering teacher in school who wasn't your average math nerd, and one day he came to class and put a bunch of Greek letters on the board; then he set up a tripod and surveyor's transit in the middle of the stage.

"This is a theodolite," he said. "It's a combination of a level and a transit. A basic form was invented in Europe in the sixteenth century. The origin of its name isn't completely clear, but we imagine it comes from the greek *thea,* 'a seeing,' *hodos,* 'a way,' *litos,* 'plain or smooth.' An instrument that helps us to see a plain, smooth way." He went on to talk about the technical aspects, but I felt suspended in a kind of clarity. Seeing a plain, smooth way. It seemed a way to proceed through difficulties. It seemed a way to live.

At work, when I looked into the theodolite, which magnified everything in its field about thirty times, I was aware of encapsulating distance, of being able to make a leap from here to there simply by putting my eye to the transit. I wished we could leap over the rest of the pregnancy and land on the other side of birth. I tried to imagine Sarah and the baby and myself as a little family. I pushed my doubts aside and went forward. It was the only thing to do.

We moved Sarah's things into my apartment, and her total belongings consisted of clothes to sing or waitress in, a few books about music and composition theory, records and an ancient record player that I was careful not to joke about, and a large assortment of fake books that included all those old torch songs she loved.

During our short engagement I worried that Sarah might backpedal and say she couldn't get married. Of course her pregnancy had precipitated all this, but once I got used to the idea, I had a sense of mission: I would protect her and make a home for us. She was nervous about miscarrying, and said the first three months were the most tenuous, which was why she didn't want everyone to know—although of course Bernard did, and I'm sure my mother told my sister. Sometimes I was scared that she would lose the baby and call everything off. Once, when she was insisting I not tell the guys at work, I even asked:

"Sarah, if something did happen, to the baby I mean, would you still go through with this?"

She looked at me as if I'd hit her. "Yes," she said quietly. "I would. What about you?"

"Yes." I hadn't thought she would misunderstand. "Yes."

We got married at the courthouse. Bernard, who I'd met only once before the wedding, cheerfully called himself her maid of honor, although he did not wear a dress. My younger brother stood up for me. My mother, my sister, and her family came, and then we went back to my mother's house where the guests started arriving almost as soon as we did. My mother had been cooking for days. She'd made our cake to Sarah's shy specifications, and Sarah kept thanking her, flushed and excited. My sister had set up a big decorated table on the patio for presents, and we were given a ton of stuff that we actually needed to set up house, and much that we didn't.

At one point in the party, Sarah came up to me holding a little crystal bird in her hand.

"Look at this," she said. "It's from your dentist, I think. He made me open it. It's so perfect." She held the small bird up to the light and gazed into it like a crystal ball.

"My mother must have told him you sing."

"I can't believe all these presents. I know it's stupid, I don't mean it to sound crass, but all this stuff makes getting married seem so real." She looked happy. I put my arms around her still-slender waist. Standing under the streamers, watching her blush with that songbird in her hand, I felt enveloped in a light and fluid happiness, a sense that everything would be all right.

We settled into the business of being pregnant, although the idea of an actual baby between us still seemed, at times, intangible. Sarah had tried to quit smoking, but she would periodically rant through the apartment saying she would kill for a cigarette. I didn't want to nag her. I was aware that, in most ways, my life was much the same. I could eat and drink whatever I wanted. I didn't feel queasy or tired. In those first weeks of marriage, we didn't really get to see each other much. I'd get home from work around six, and she'd already left for her waitressing job, the dinner shift. She was home by midnight, but by then I was usually asleep. I tried to stay up, but I was tired from being out in the sun all day.

The sex between us disappeared for a while. If I woke up when she came to bed and started to touch her, she'd take my hand and whisper in my ear. "You have no idea how tired I am. If you touch my breasts I'll kill you." I tried to be enlightened; I knew it was a phase. My sister had given her copy of *What to Expect When You're Expecting* and I'd looked up "Intercourse" and other things in the index, so I knew her breasts were sore, her fatigue was real. I tried, on nights when she was gone, to sit down and read the book methodically, but it gave me the willies. The pictures of babies in early pregnancy seemed scarily unformed. When I flipped forward to the pictures of the ninth month, the baby inside that penciled torso seemed a colossal imposition on the inside of a woman's body.

After Sarah quit smoking, she said she was calmer than she'd ever been in her life, but sometimes things set her off, things I never saw coming.

One gray Saturday we made love and slept late. We talked about going to look for a crib, but neither of us had the energy to tackle shopping on a Saturday afternoon. I sat down on the sofa and clicked on the remote. Sarah had been sitting in the easy chair on the other side of the room and she got out of the chair and headed for the bedroom.

"Hey, where are you going?"

"I hate sports."

"Why?"

"I just hate the television being on in the background. I can't read. This is the only really comfortable place to sit."

I hit Mute and patted the sofa next to me. "Come over here. Can't you think of it as a comforting sound, kind of a happy background noise?"

She shook her head. "It reminds me of my stepfather."

I clicked it off. "Well, what about him?"

"Oh, it's no big story. Although my mother did marry him twice, so that's something." She stood in the middle of the living room. I waited for her to continue. Finally, she came back and sat next to me on the couch. "He wasn't mean to me or anything. As a matter of fact, that was it. He wasn't anything. He acted like I was some handicap you couldn't mention. My mother used to feed me dinner before he came home so they could eat by themselves. I had to wait in my room, alone, while they ate. It seemed to take forever. I don't think she told him about me until after they'd been dating for a while, and then she kind of sprung me on him."

"What do you mean she married him twice?"

"Well, they split up when I was about eleven or twelve, and then we really had no money. I guess my mother got on assistance, I don't know. She started going out with this other guy then, Ernesto, and our place was so small, there was no hiding me. He knew about me from the start. He was a really nice man and he told my mother . . ." and she stopped, her voice wavered. "He told my mother that she should marry him. He had dental insurance at his job and he would get me braces. It was like the nicest thing anyone ever wanted to do for me." Sarah turned her face away, but her voice sounded choked and thin. "He was real diplomatic about it. He was afraid of hurting my feelings, but I knew my teeth were crooked. We had a mirror for Chrissakes. Oh, I prayed that she would marry him, but she didn't. I don't know why." Then Sarah really started to sob, a heaving kind of crying she'd never let me hear before. I held her for a few minutes, until she caught her breath. "And then we were really broke again, and my stepfather showed up, and my mother married him again."

She leaned her head against my shoulder and wept. I smoothed her hair. Until I met Sarah, I had never thought of myself as naive, but every time I learned something new about her, I realized how foolishly simple my constructs were, what little comfort I could offer.

"What about your real father?"

"Yeah, I asked about him once."

"What did your mother say?"

"She wasn't sure who he was."

I brushed a wet strand of hair from her face.

"Sometimes it kills me to think there's someone out there who doesn't even know I exist. I mean, chances are, knowing my mother's taste, he probably wouldn't care. But I do think about it. All these people in the world who are dying to have kids and can't get pregnant . . . what if my actual father is someone like that? And I'll never know. It's not like I'm adopted and there's an actual record. My mother was probably dating a couple guys, trying to figure out who'd be the best bet."

"This baby will know who I am."

"I know." She touched my cheek.

Sarah seemed to escape without morning sickness, but as her body grew and changed, her moods did too. I came home from work one night to find the remnants of cigarette smoke drifting in the air.

"Hey." I kissed her on the cheek and flopped down in a chair, deliberately casual. "How're you?"

"Not so good."

"Did you have a cigarette?"

"Yes, and I feel crappy about it. But sometimes I just can't stand it: no caffeine, no junk, no preservatives. My nose is all stuffed up and I can't take cold medicine. I've had a headache for days and I can't even take aspirin."

"There must be something you can take."

"No, there isn't. Read the damn book!" She hurled the heavy paperback at the wall, and it fell, ruffling to the floor. "Caffeine can cause birth defects. One little aspirin could be disaster. I can't even shit I'm so blocked up. God, I'm only starting to show and I feel like a cow. This is awful. I don't know what's wrong with me."

"There's nothing wrong with you. You're pregnant."

"I've tried to read all those sprout-head books. Breast-feeding, natural childbirth. I wish I could be like those women, but I can't. I'm not like that."

"You don't have to be *like* anything. You're not required to buy a pair of Birkenstocks and wear purple before you have a baby."

She laughed soundlessly and leaned against me. For a moment I was pleased, but I sensed this was only the beginning.

Sarah seemed to go from barely looking pregnant to being a full-on, pregnant lady almost overnight. I loved how her skin felt, the softness of her, but Sarah was unappeased.

"You start looking at jeans ads on television and thinking: I'll never look like that again," she said. "And all of a sudden, men don't even notice you. It's like you're invisible."

"You'll go back to the way you were."

The phone rang and Sarah reached for it. She was quiet for a full minute, and then her face brightened.

"Yeah, yeah, oh God, that'd be great."

I couldn't decipher what she might be talking about. She paced the length of the short telephone cord, her voice high and questioning. All of a sudden, she stopped. She stared at her reflection in the sliding glass door.

"When is the place opening up? Oh Bernard, oh shit, I can't. Imagine what I'll look like. Oh this is awful. You haven't seen me in three weeks. I've gone from being a little, I don't know, thicker, to being . . . well, pregnant. Oh God. Look, can I call you back? Don't say anything to your friend yet, okay?"

She hung up the phone.

"A friend of Bernard's is opening up a supper club in Santa Barbara. A really nice place. They're going to have music and Bernard mentioned me. Actually, the owner heard me sing about a year ago and they want to book me as the club's opening act.

But they won't be opening for at least eight weeks. How can I do it? I mean, I can still sing, but a pregnant singer? I'd be absurd. Oh, I can't stand it!"

"Couldn't you work there after the baby is born?" I knew it was weak, even as I said it.

"It won't be the same. This could be my one chance and—"

"Sarah—"

"I really can't talk about this now." She ran into the bedroom and slammed the door behind her.

It was as if I'd come around a bend in the road and saw a long downward grade. Sarah stayed in the bedroom all evening. I made her tea, tried to bring her food, but she told me to stay out. Finally, when I wanted to sleep, I tried the knob. The door swung open and I went in and lay down beside her. Her face was swollen. She had cried herself to sleep without getting out of her clothes. I took off her shoes and socks, helped her get under the sheets. In her half-awakeness she clung to me and cried again.

I tried to be hopeful, but often when I came home, she would be playing albums on her ancient stereo, and I knew from the music what she was feeling: Etta James, Nina Simone, pain like a fast-moving river underground. She had an old bootleg album of Nina Simone's in a plain white cover, and those scratchy songs held the purest kind of longing I had ever heard.

Once Sarah started weeping in the middle of making dinner.

"I'll never be a singer now," she said.

"Oh come on, don't think like that."

"You really have no idea. Babies take time. They need you. It's years and years and years of wiping noses and butts. And by the time they don't need you to do that anymore, you're old and you've made this huge space in your life for them, and they just walk out through it."

There was little I could say. We started going to childbirth classes, and on the first night they showed us a movie of labor and birth. The woman in the movie lowed in pain; she seemed enormous and powerless.

Sarah leaned over to me and whispered. "This is awful. They should show this movie to high school kids instead of distributing condoms."

I squeezed her hand. We both giggled about the couples who

kept talking about videotaping their births. The classes brought us closer together for a while and I could see that Sarah was really trying to keep her spirits up. She told me she lingered in New Age–type bookstores; the atmosphere made her feel positive: all that floaty music and people getting past their problems.

Making love had changed again. Sarah was so big that there was much we couldn't do.

"I don't like how I look, so I don't see how you can."

"It is different," I admitted. "Just gives me some new places to explore."

I kissed her foot, her ankle, the backs of her knees. It was a Sunday afternoon. In the beginning, we'd done most of our lovemaking at night or in early morning half-light, but now, because of fatigue, daytime seemed best.

"What are these?" I'd noticed them before: small pinkish circles on the backs of her thighs.

"Ringworm." She lay on her back to hide them.

"Boy, you're getting gritty in your pregnant state." I put my hand on her hip and pushed her onto her side.

"Paul, stop it."

I touched the small pink circles. Scars. I pictured Sarah that first night at the beach, the glowing ember in the dark she had quashed underfoot. I felt a terrible heat inside me.

"Who did this?" I demanded. "Who?"

"My mother." She muffled the words into the pillow, as if pushing back a scream. Then she pushed herself up off the bed. "I really can't talk about this."

"How old were you? How could she do this?"

But she wouldn't say anything else.

Sarah wanted Bernard to be at the birth, which was fine with me. I was nervous about being the one who was supposed to be calm and supportive. I liked Bernard. He'd had us over for dinner a few times and made some really nice meals. He didn't treat me like some hulking hetero that had gotten his nightingale knocked up. Although Bernard wasn't that much older than us, I felt as if I'd passed some kind of parent-approval test when Sarah told me that Bernard thought I was "adorable and very solid." Apparently he thought I was a little rough around the edges, but with a little cleaning up, Bernard thought I "could be very *GQ*." I supposed this was a compliment.

As it turned out, Bernard achieved a kind of heroic stature in my mind. Nothing in our classes prepared me for the unadorned fear I felt during Sarah's labor and delivery, and Bernard presented himself as the soul of calm and restraint as we held Sarah's hands, and gazed at each other, fearfully, over her head.

Sarah woke up with cramps one morning, and asked me to stay home from work. We had made a birthing plan, as they'd insisted in the class, and she didn't want to go to the hospital until it really seemed necessary. We walked around old-town Ventura in the sunshine, ate some ice cream, and basically puttered around until early afternoon when she said she wanted to go home. Her requests were simple and understated, but I obeyed her with the precision of a marshal. By the time we got back to the apartment, Sarah said, "Beep Bernard. Call the doctor. In that order."

The women who taught the birthing classes had tried to prepare us for all kinds of scenarios, and I'd expected, given Sarah's temperament, a certain amount of cursing and yelling, but nothing prepared me for her abject stance in the face of prolonged pain. Her labor went on all night, into morning, and yet, when I tried to recall when different things happened, or were done to her, I can't. Everything went by in a helpless blur. Toward the end she said she was dying, she couldn't do it anymore; I'd seen more blood come out of her than I'd ever have believed possible, and I felt at the perimeter of some terrible kind of hell in life. I held her hand, stroked her hair. Nothing I said could even approach being enough. Sarah had been pushing for what seemed like forever. The blood vessels near her eyes had burst. Finally the doctor said that he was going to use forceps, and if that didn't work, they would have to do a C-section. The doctor explained it calmly, but he was clearly in a hurry.

"Forceps?" she said weakly. She put her head down on the pillow. "No, no. One more try."

And one more push set everything in motion. "Sarah, Sarah, Sarah, it's coming, it's going to be all right," I murmured into her hair. I didn't even look at the baby at first. I didn't want to let go of Sarah's hand. When they put the baby on top of her, tiny and bluish, I didn't even care if it was a boy or a girl. I wanted to cover them both with my body and weep.

Sarah stayed in the hospital for two days. Both of her eyes were darkened; she looked as if she'd been punched in the face. The baby was a girl. Sarah insisted on naming her Nina, and even though the name reminded me of all those sad songs, I thought that, after what Sarah had been through, she could name the baby anything she wanted. Nurses came in and out to bring the baby to her for feeding, but it didn't go very well. Little Nina was groggy from the birth taking so long; she didn't seem to know how to suck. Then, hungry and impatient, she wailed a tiny thin cry that seemed puny against the world. Lactation specialists and nurses came and went. Sarah pointed out that everyone knew how to handle her breasts except the baby. They assured her it was all right, that nursing would work out.

Sarah's milk came in the day we took the baby home. She woke up from a nap to find her breasts so tight and swollen that it hurt to raise her arms.

"Bring her to me," she said. "See if she'll nurse."

The baby was sleeping and I hated to disturb her, but I didn't want to contradict Sarah. I set her in Sarah's arms, and the baby bumped her blind and tiny head against Sarah's breast, which was so hard and swollen that the baby couldn't get enough nipple in her mouth to make it work.

"Oh God, this hurts, this hurts. My breasts feel like grapefruits. You can't believe it."

I placed my hand under her other breast. It was heavy, hot and tight, the skin underneath had a hard, rumpled feeling. "Oh, this hurts so much," Sarah whimpered.

The baby, half-awake now, was crying, angry.

Helpless during the past few days, I had been reading the baby books diligently. I picked the baby up. "Go take a hot shower. See if you can get a little out." Sarah obediently went off toward the bathroom. The baby wailed, and I tried to bounce her gently like my mother did, but little Nina was pissed off and hungry and didn't appreciate the ride. I stood outside the bathroom door and over the water I heard Sarah sobbing in the rain.

Sarah tried, oh she tried. The baby finally did learn to nurse, and when she finally got the hang of it, she sucked so hard that Sarah's nipples became sore and cracked. Sarah wept whenever she put the baby to her breast.

"Sarah, this is crazy. I know this is supposed to be the best thing, but if it hurts this much it can't be right."

"I *am* doing it right."

"I don't mean it like that—right for you. It's too much."

"I've got to do this. I don't want to be like my mother."

"Giving up nursing doesn't mean you're going to be like your mother."

"I want to do better."

"You are, sweetheart, you are."

The first two weeks of little Nina's existence were the longest two weeks of my life. Almost every evening, my mother came over after work and cooked and did laundry. It seemed unbelievable that it took all of us to cope with such a tiny being. Before Nina was born, I had imagined that we'd put her to bed in the evening, and then Sarah and I would sit down and relax, maybe eat together. Sarah was right. I had no idea.

After two weeks, Sarah got a fever and chills. The doctor told her it was a breast infection and she finally gave up nursing. We started giving the baby formula and Sarah cried in my mother's arms.

"I'm a bad mother already. The most basic thing and I can't do it."

"Oh shush." My mother, sitting next to Sarah on the couch, held her and rocked her. "None of us nursed babies thirty years ago, and they turned out fine. Look at Paul. You did your best. Shush."

One thing about the formula was that the baby actually slept. Sometimes four hours in a row. We'd sit out on the patio, and the sunlight through the pines and the smell of eucalyptus in the air was healing. Nina was peaceful and we gazed at her and marveled at her tiny perfections.

Just when I thought we'd gotten past the worst, the colic started. I remember the exact night, a Thursday. Nina started crying around four in the afternoon, and she cried so piercingly and angrily that we were sure something terrible was wrong. We phoned my mother, who had been planning to give herself a night off, and she came over. She picked up Nina, felt her little stomach, watched her legs kick. "Gas," she said. "It's just gas." On the second night I looked up *colic* in the baby book. When I read aloud that it could last for three months, Sarah put her head on my shoulder and wept. We tried a pacifier, which helped for about two minutes; we turned her on her stomach and rolled her gently on our knees; we wrapped her tightly in blankets and held her; we gave her baths; we tried a bottle, which she wouldn't drink; and I held her on my shoulder and walked back and forth, back and forth, in our small apartment. Sarah and I started to bicker. We couldn't help it. Whenever one of us tried a new and ineffective remedy, the other had just thought of something different that might work. Taking Nina out for a drive was the one thing that seemed to help. Her screaming became a horrible kind of clockwork. Every afternoon around four she would start, and she wailed until 11:30 or twelve. I came home from work and looked down at her little body, kicking and screaming. She seemed, at times, malevolent.

"There's some kind of hormone you secrete when you're nursing," Sarah said. "It's supposed to make you more patient. Sometimes I look at her and I just want to smash her. It's awful. She's so tiny, it would be so easy to hurt her." Sarah's eyes filled with tears.

"Sarah, lots of people must feel like that," but I felt a kind of queasy unsureness. The baby's yelling drove me crazy too, but I didn't want to hurt her.

"I think about how easily she could break. I'm not even very strong and I could hurt her without hardly trying." Sarah started to sob.

"Look, I'll take the baby out for a drive. You stay here and try to rest."

Sarah nodded and I picked the baby up and carried her out to the car. The night was clear, the stars sharp, I saw Orion above me. I got in the car and headed for the freeway. Nina's crying drove me crazy too, but her delicacy seemed a kind of protective coating. She couldn't help yelling; her stomach hurt. It was probably because of the formula. I thought about the burns on Sarah's legs. Had Sarah's mother done it just because she could?

As I drove, and the baby was soothed, I tried to imagine us past all of this: I saw Sarah, with Nina in her stroller, walking down a hill near the Mission in Ventura. Sarah paused to light a cigarette, lifting her hand, her wrist bent to shield the lighted match, and in that moment the stroller slipped from her grasp and began to glide down the hill. A second too late, Sarah grasped the air after it. The image began to haunt me: Sarah holding a cigarette in her delicate lips, that moment of lifting her hand with the lighted match. It played over and over in my head. She wouldn't let anything happen to Nina, I said it aloud, but a tiny doubt twisted inside me.

When I woke up the following Saturday, the blinds were half-drawn, but I saw the brightness outside. It was late. The apartment was still. Sarah wasn't in bed. The unexpected quiet made me swing out of bed with a jolt of fear. I ran into the baby's room and saw Nina, asleep on her back, her arms tossed above her head in a baby's abandonment to sleep. I stood there, watching to make sure the blanket rose and fell, filled with that terrible hesitation I felt every time I checked on her sleeping form.

I walked into the kitchen and saw the note on the kitchen table.

Dear Paul,

Don't come after me. This is better—I think you know that. I won't be the kind of mother I want to be, and I can't live with being like my mother. Please know that I really do love you, both of you. Please tell Nina that I really, really did try.

Love,
Sarah

I stood there for a long moment; the note was too simple to encompass everything we'd been through. It couldn't be real. I walked into the living room. The stereo was gone.

I felt as if the past months had been a long and precarious exercise in keeping myself in check—in being calm, soothing, trying to say the right thing. Clearly I hadn't done enough. I felt, rather than heard, a kind of roaring in my ears, and through it I heard the thin sound of Nina crying in her crib. I went to her room and when I picked her up she was soaked, so I changed her diaper and put on one of the million tiny outfits we had, and carried her into the kitchen to warm up a bottle of formula.

I mumbled to her while I heated it up, and when it was right, I grabbed a cloth diaper and went to sit in the living room and feed her. In the sunlight, I saw the fine starlike wrinkles on her knuckles, the way the light shone orange-red through her ear, the delicacy of her tiny, greedy mouth. She was oblivious to everything.

When she was done eating, I tried to burp her, and she threw up all over my shirt and herself, missing the diaper I'd so confidently placed on my shoulder. I changed her clothes again and carried her out to the patio. From our little deck, fringed by pines, I couldn't quite see the ocean; the freeway was in the way. I thought of Sarah, and guessed that she was heading north, back to that rainy place she came from. She had said she would never lie to me, and I knew what she'd said in her note was true. She did not want me to come after her. I thought about how only the road would connect us, an imaginary filament she rode away on. I thought of the uncertainty I'd felt in those days at work, how I kept telling myself that everything would work out. For a brief time it had seemed that everything came into focus with the clarity of possibility, as if looking through a lens, I had captured something true and real. But my vision was deceptive; I hadn't taken into account what lay beyond the scope of the lens. Looking down at Nina, I wondered how I would explain her mother's departure. And knowing then that I was truly all she had in the world, I felt something vast and fearful inside me break open. How could I protect her? She was so tiny and perfect and we had failed her already. It must have scared her as I wept for my inchoate and helpless love, for the scars on Sarah's legs, for all she did not tell me. When Nina was old enough to ask, how would I explain it all? What could I possibly say that would be sweet and also true? I thought of the party my mother threw for us, Sarah happy and shining with the crystal bird in her hand, and how, in spite of our failing, I could say at least that she was truly borne in love. I knew it would seem very little. I hoped it would be enough.

The Iowa Short Fiction Award and John Simmons Short Fiction Award Winners

2000
Articles of Faith, Elizabeth Oness
Judge: Elizabeth McCracken

2000
Troublemakers, John McNally
Judge: Elizabeth McCracken

1999
House Fires, Nancy Reisman
Judge: Marilynne Robinson

1999
Out of the Girls' Room and into the Night, Thisbe Nissen
Judge: Marilynne Robinson

1998
The River of Lost Voices,
Mark Brazaitis
Judge: Stuart Dybek

1998
Friendly Fire,
Kathryn Chetkovich
Judge: Stuart Dybek

1997
Thank You for Being Concerned and Sensitive, Jim Henry
Judge: Ann Beattie

1997
Within the Lighted City,
Lisa Lenzo
Judge: Ann Beattie

1996
Hints of His Mortality,
David Borofka
Judge: Oscar Hijuelos

1996
Western Electric,
Don Zancanella
Judge: Oscar Hijuelos

1995
Listening to Mozart,
Charles Wyatt
Judge: Ethan Canin

1995
May You Live in Interesting Times, Tereze Glück
Judge: Ethan Canin

1994
The Good Doctor,
Susan Onthank Mates
Judge: Joy Williams

1994
Igloo among Palms,
Rod Val Moore
Judge: Joy Williams

1993
Happiness, Ann Harleman
Judge: Francine Prose

1993
Macauley's Thumb,
Lex Williford
Judge: Francine Prose

1993
Where Love Leaves Us,
Renée Manfredi
Judge: Francine Prose

1992
My Body to You,
Elizabeth Searle
Judge: James Salter

1992
Imaginary Men, Enid Shomer
Judge: James Salter

1991
The Ant Generator,
Elizabeth Harris
Judge: Marilynne Robinson

1991
Traps, Sondra Spatt Olsen
Judge: Marilynne Robinson

1990
A Hole in the Language,
Marly Swick
Judge: Jayne Anne Phillips

1989
Lent: The Slow Fast,
Starkey Flythe, Jr.
Judge: Gail Godwin

1989
Line of Fall, Miles Wilson
Judge: Gail Godwin

1988
The Long White,
Sharon Dilworth
Judge: Robert Stone

1988
The Venus Tree,
Michael Pritchett
Judge: Robert Stone

1987
Fruit of the Month, Abby Frucht
Judge: Alison Lurie

1987
Star Game, Lucia Nevai
Judge: Alison Lurie

1986
Eminent Domain,
Dan O'Brien
Judge: Iowa Writers'
Workshop

1986
Resurrectionists,
Russell Working
Judge: Tobias Wolff

1985
Dancing in the Movies,
Robert Boswell
Judge: Tim O'Brien

1984
Old Wives' Tales,
Susan M. Dodd
Judge: Frederick Busch

1983
Heart Failure, Ivy Goodman
Judge: Alice Adams

1982
Shiny Objects,
Dianne Benedict
Judge: Raymond Carver

1981
The Phototropic Woman,
Annabel Thomas
Judge: Doris Grumbach

1980
Impossible Appetites,
James Fetler
Judge: Francine du Plessix
Gray

1979
Fly Away Home, Mary Hedin
Judge: John Gardner

1978
A Nest of Hooks, Lon Otto
Judge: Stanley Elkin

1977
The Women in the Mirror,
Pat Carr
Judge: Leonard Michaels

1976
The Black Velvet Girl,
C. E. Poverman
Judge: Donald Barthelme

1975
Harry Belten and the Mendelssohn Violin Concerto,
Barry Targan
Judge: George P. Garrett

1974
After the First Death There Is No Other, Natalie L. M. Petesch
Judge: William H. Gass

1973
The Itinerary of Beggars,
H. E. Francis
Judge: John Hawkes

1972
The Burning and Other Stories, Jack Cady
Judge: Joyce Carol Oates

1971
Old Morals, Small Continents, Darker Times,
Philip F. O'Connor
Judge: George P. Elliott

1970
The Beach Umbrella,
Cyrus Colter
Judges: Vance Bourjaily and Kurt Vonnegut, Jr.

Joel Iannuzzi

Elizabeth Oness lives in La Crosse, Wisconsin, with her husband, the poet C. Mikal Oness, and their son. She directs marketing and development for Sutton Hoo Press. Her stories have received numerous honors, including an O. Henry Prize and a Nelson Algren Award. She has recently completed her first novel, *Twelve Rivers of the Body*.